MIDNIGHT SPARKS

EMMANUELLE

USA TODAY BESTSELLING AUTHOR

SNOW

Smart Lily
Publishing

CARTER HILLS BAND UNIVERSE
(SUGGESTED READING ORDER)

Carter Hills Band series
False Promises

HEART SONG DUET
Blindsided
Forevermore

Whiskey Melody series
Sweet Agony

SECOND TEAR DUET
Cruel Destiny
Beautiful Salvation

BREATHLESS DUET
Wild Encounter
Brittle Scars

Upon A Star series
Last Hope

Midnight Sparks

Love Song For Two series
<u>Lonesome Heart Duet</u>
Fallen Legend
Rising Star

<u>Two of Us Duet</u>
Snowbound

Wicked Love

All titles available at
emmanuellesnow.com

For the best experience, read in the order as shown above

WHAT THE REVIEWS SAY

- "Another wallop of a fun read where the pages twirled as if they were tinsel." **(Book Reviews by Shalini)**

- "This book is a perfect Christmas read filled with passion, steamy romance, humour and drama." **(Priya Bookstagram)**

- "I love this author's writing so much. It's captivating and pretty. I feel so happy when I'm reading her books." **(Jessica Belmont blog)**

- "It was funny emotional and sizzling at the same time. It's not my first book by Emmanuelle Snow and it certainly will not be my last." **(Goodreads review)**

- "This is a book in The Carter Hills Band Series and it is Aisha and Gavin's story and omg it is definitely a must read." **(Jean, Amazon UK)**

- "I am constantly falling in love with that characters that Emmanuelle creates within the Carter Hills Band world, and Aisha and Gavin are no different. This story warmed my heart, and I was so engrossed in the story I never wanted to put it down." (**Angelica, Goodreads**)

- "This story is one you won't want to put down." (**Abigail, Goodreads**)

TRIGGER WARNINGS

Disclaimer

My books are realistic and emotional love stories.
I'm an advocate for mental health, and some topics could
be sensitive for certain readers since they are portrayed as
close to real life as possible.

I've listed the potential trigger warnings for each title on
my website.

Be advised that those trigger warnings could potentially be
spoiler alerts for the storylines.

Those sensitive topics have been written with the utmost
care and respect. Please reach out if you have questions or
comments.

All books contain sexuality, mature content, and language
not intended for people under 18 years of age.

For other readers' sake, please avoid spoilers in your
reviews.

Thank you and have a wonderful day!

Emmanuelle

emmanuellesnow.com

Christmas is one of my favorite times of the year. To all of you who crave the music, the festivities, the precious family moments, the movies, and the love: cheers!

To Abigail, Angelica, Becky, Elayne, Hazel, Jean, Melissa, Miriam, Nicole, Shalini, and Tanja.
With all my love and grateful heart.

BECOME A VIP

TO NEVER MISS A THING

Snow's VIP

Join **Emmanuelle Snow's VIP newsletter** for all the cool stuff, promos, new releases, giveaways, and gifts.

emmanuellesnow.com

Snow's Soulmates

Join Emmanuelle Snow's Facebook VIP group, **Snow's Soulmates**, to chat with her and other readers, get updates, and more bonus content.

facebook.com/groups/snowvip

STARS AND SNOWFLAKES
THE SONG

In the silence of the night, I wish
    you could be here with me
Looking at the falling snowflakes, I
    walk this old country road by
    myself
In the silence of the night, I tread
    home, hoping you'd be there
    waiting for me
But I know better. It's Christmas
    Eve, and you're far away
    from here
And I know Christmas will never be
    the same if I can't have you in
    my arms tonight

[CHORUS]

My footprints in the snow are
    tracing a path for you to follow
My heart, sizzling in the cold night

darkness, is waiting for you like a
    fire warm caress
The frost on my lips missed the heat
    of you when we kiss
The stars in the sky are a light,
    promising you everything will be
    all right
Please come back to me, please
    come home to me
Tomorrow it's Christmas Day,
    tomorrow is only a few
    hours away

In my head, I write a thousand love
    songs you'll never hear
Looking at the falling snowflakes, I
    wish the night could heal our
    hearts
In my head, I pray I could erase the
    words I said the last time you
    were here
My heart is broken in half when
    you're not around
Please Christmas, make all my
    wishes come true
Maybe it could show me the way
    back to you

[CHORUS]
Snowflakes stop falling, and the
    clouds melt in the sky
A shiver runs through me, and I
    stare upward, wishing for a sign

Snowflakes stop falling, and the stars
    shine high
That's when I know you've never
    left me
That's when I'm sure you'll be there
    when I get home
Waiting for me by the Christmas
    tree, waiting for me to make you
    my own

[CHORUS]
I can't believe you're still here, this
    was my biggest wish this year
My heart will forever belong to you,
    you and I, we're up for a
    long ride
Merry Christmas, baby, Merry
    Christmas, to you
Whenever you have doubts, wish for
    stars and snowflakes in the sky
Whenever you have doubts, I'll hold
    your hand and stay by your side

Music and lyrics by Aisha Jones and Gavin Moore

Chapter 1
Aisha

I threw in my black heels and zipped up my suitcase. I was so done. Nothing could keep me here—not even the holidays, especially the ones at the end of the year. I hated everything about Christmas. The cheer. The smiles from strangers. The camaraderie. And don't get me started on those cookies and carols. God, those were the worst. Whoever invented the holiday traditions must have done it as a sick joke. And now the entire freaking world was obsessed with them. Well done, champ.

With one last glance around my bedroom, I made sure I had everything I needed for this trip. Two weeks on an island in the middle of the Caribbean Sea, with an open bar and palm trees. I knew I had packed the right outfits.

Little black dress that made my legs look longer. *Check.*

Sparkling red dress that gave my boobs all the attention they deserved. *Check.*

Sunblock, shades, and hat. *Check. Check. And check.*

Oh yes, the tiny white string bikini I could flaunt my curves in. *Check too.*

My phone buzzed. Of course, it was my manager. I rolled my eyes because I didn't even have to look to know what the message said.

RILEY

Did you change your mind about that holiday special in Times Square?

Laughter rose in my chest and burst free, echoing louder than it should have. As if Riley didn't know better. I didn't do Christmas shows. Never. He knew it. But that didn't stop him from trying to convince me.

Every single year.

ME

Forget it. And Carter or whoever else you want me to sing a duet with. No special appearance. Me + island = perfect vacation. Talk to you next year, Ry.

RILEY

If you change your mind, kiddo, you know where to find me.

ME

Sorry. Not happening.

RILEY

Fine. Didn't hurt to try. Maybe someday you'll actually say yes to me. Keeping my fingers crossed.

ME

In your dreams. But I love you for looking out for me. Have a blast with Santa and his bunch of stupid elves.

In the entryway, I slid my phone into the back pocket

of my jeans, and adjusting my lacy black top, I perused my image in the mirror, debating whether to let my hair loose or not. This morning, I woke up early to straighten my black curls. It took me over an hour to get them to behave. I gathered my hair into a ponytail, held it for a second, then let it fall. Hair down it was. With one sweep, I colored my lips in ruby red—*Passion red*, they called it—suiting my dark complexion perfectly, and applied a thick coat of mascara to the lashes framing my dark kohl-lined eyes. From a hook behind the door, I grabbed my jacket, the one matching my lipstick, and got the hell out of my house before someone else tried to change my mind.

Last year, I went to Fiji for the holidays. The year before, I traveled to the wildest parts of Australia. I chose my destinations with a single goal in mind: anywhere I could fade from sight for two weeks. This year, I had chosen Playa De La Isla Azul, a small island in the Caribbean Sea, with a population of less than two thousand and a handful of resorts. It was so small that planes only landed there once or twice a week. Someone on my last tour recommended it, and I had decided to give it a try. It was exactly the kind of place where someone could disappear for a while.

The cab driver climbed out of the car to grab my suitcase and stuffed it in the trunk. With careful steps, I tried not to get too much snow into my shoes. Sure, golden heels weren't the most convenient to walk in Tennessee at this time of the year, but they made me feel powerful. And sexy. So be damned the frost bites. My toes could suffer until we reached the airport.

The cab pulled away. Out the back window, my house grew smaller, its roof and front yard dusted with a thin layer of snow. I let out a long, slow sigh. My shoulders relaxed with each mile away as I sank into the seat, the tension in my upper back dissolving and excitement unfurling in the pit of my stomach. Yes, I was long overdue for a vacation, and more than ready to let the good times roll.

The driver turned the radio on, and a Christmas song I knew too well drifted through the air, filling the space around me.

With a roll of my eyes and doing my best to avoid grimacing, I pleaded to the driver, "I'll give you an extra tip—fifty bucks—if you turn that damn thing off right now."

Our gazes met in the rearview mirror.

"You serious?"

"Dead serious." I flashed him a grin, just for good measure.

"Fine. The lady wins," he agreed with a wink. I sighed. I couldn't wait to be out of here. He droned on, "You're not a fan of the holidays as I can see. I thought singers like you, the ones singing love songs for a living, fancied all things romantic. Forget Valentine's Day, Christmas is the real deal. The most romantic time of the year."

"Well, people like me don't all enjoy this shit. It's over-rated. Commercial. Full of clichés. No, thanks. I'll choose palm trees over candy canes any day."

"You'd be surprised how the holidays can win you over."

I snorted. "Don't think so."

With earbuds in, I slumped in my seat, watching the Nashville skyline through the window as it disappeared, the more we neared the airport.

Chapter 2

Aisha

"Can I get you anything to drink? Eggnog? We offer it for a limited time. Our Christmas special," the stewardess recited, her perfectly painted red lips offering me a warm smile, her blonde hair curled to perfection, and the glint—that Christmas cheer too many people bore during this time of the year—enveloping her in an aura.

"Thanks," I said, returning her smile. "I don't do Christmas. I'll have a dirty martini. Three olives."

"I'll be right back." She walked away with a frown, offering the couple sitting before me the eggnog, her over-enthusiastic still plastered grin on.

Once I drowned my martini, I slept through the rest of the flight, the music coming from my earbuds soothing my annoyed self.

We landed in Playa De La Isla Azul four hours later. Through the airplane window, I admired the azure ocean, sparkling under the sun's rays as if it were filled with billions of diamonds.

I breathed in calm and happiness.

Yes, this was what I longed for. A vacation under the sun.

In the small airport, I spotted the lone Christmas tree in a corner and a medium-sized wreath near the baggage claim carousel.

I breathed out my relief.

These people weren't Christmas fanatics.

Even better.

Up to now, everything was more than fine. Exactly what I'd hoped for.

I turned my phone back on, and the notification chimes went off, informing me I had four unread messages and six missed calls. Great. I had only been gone for a few hours, and already people were looking for me.

RILEY

Aisha, why is Scooter not with you?

I gritted my teeth. Scooter was my bodyguard. The one guy I usually brought along each time I left Nashville or went to events. One of the perks of my fame, if it could be considered a perk. *Oopsy.* I cringed. Riley would be mad— so freaking much. But how could I blame him? He always looked out for his artists. And I loved him for it… Usually. This time I wanted to be on my own. Breathe the air far from everyone else.

RILEY

Aisha, don't ignore me. Scooter informed me you left without telling him. You should know better. When I'm pissed, it isn't good for anyone. Pick up. Or text me back.

MOM

> Beta, where are you? Call me when you have a minute. Auntie Barbs is knitting everyone her traditional Christmas sweaters, and she wants to know if you prefer it in deep green or forest green.

RILEY

> Aisha Jones. Call me ASAP or I'll come get you myself.

I clamped my lips shut, fighting the scream clawing its way up my throat, ready to rip through the air and pierce a few eardrums. No, thank you, I didn't want a sweater. Green was so not my color. Mom, being an Indian, didn't even celebrate Christmas. And no, I didn't want Scooter to tag along this time. He had a wife and newborn twins. I might hate Christmas, but I wasn't completely heartless. No way I'd deprive them of celebrating together. As a family.

ME

> Ry, Scoot has a family. His kids need him. I'll be all right. I'm on an island. It's so small it's almost private. With a hat and shades on, nobody will give me trouble. Enjoy New York and try to take some time off for once. Kiss Devon for me.

ME

> Mom, tell Auntie Barbs thank you for the sweater, but I'll pass. She should knit herself one instead, she always forgets it. Every. Single. Year. I just landed in Playa De La Isla Azul, the non-Christmas paradise. Will keep you posted. Love ya.

Dragging my suitcases behind me, I shifted the weight of the bag on my shoulder as I entered the shuttle sent by the hotel. Perhaps shuttle wasn't the right word. The vehicle was more like an extra-long golf cart, almost the size of a mini-bus, with a white roof and all the sides completely insulated by transparent doors. I was quite taken in by the innovative design and the cooling system. What a blessing in the island heat. I dropped into a seat, watching the scenery through the window, my newfound smile hard to tame.

I couldn't wait to get to my destination.

I'd never come to this island and much less to this resort before, but the photos on their site were stunning— sunlit rooms in earthy tones, soaring ceilings, and a private deck with a breathtaking ocean view. California king beds with white fluffy comforters. Glass-walled showers big enough for ten people. Pool shaped like a clover leaf. A ribbon of white sand stretched along the coastline, kissed by the waves and stretching as far as the eye could see, dotted with tiki huts rented by the day. The resort also featured a VIP bar, a sun-dappled yoga corner tucked away in the garden, and chair massage stations I'd already booked for the length of my stay. It was the perfect place to keep a low profile and stay under the radar. Nothing could be better than that. Absolutely nothing.

I pictured heaven exactly like this.

"Welcome to Domingo Resort," a man, Pablo according to his name tag, dressed in a white uniform, his skin dark from too much time spent under the sun, greeted me when I checked in. "We're happy you chose to vacation with us." He gestured a short man forward. "Here's George. He'll carry your luggage to your room."

I acknowledged the man with a nod as he loaded my bags onto a buggy, and brought my attention back to Pablo.

"You'll be in the El Mar pavilion. Presidential suite as

requested. Separate entrance. Lots of privacy." I nodded. "Follow George. He'll show you the way. If you have any questions, press zero on the phone in your room, and it will connect you to the VIP guest service. From everyone at Domingo Resort, we hope you enjoy your stay." He handed me a welcome package, which included the magnetic key and some brochures about the island and nearby activities.

When we reached my pavilion, George grabbed the key from my hand and unlocked the door, waving me in.

The moment I entered, I held my breath and blinked a few times, surveying the space around me. It was everything I imagined it to be. And more. I clapped my hands together, unable to tame my ear-to-ear smile.

For the next hour, I settled in, hanging my precious wardrobe in the closet and organizing my toiletries and makeup in the white-tiled bathroom.

Wearing a golden and black one-piece skimpy swimsuit under a lacy black cover-up, with my shades on, I hit the beach, ready to start my vacation in style.

A woman about my mother's age stopped me when I was heading toward my designated tiki hut. "Oh, it's you. You're that country singer who won an award last month, aren't you?" She snapped her fingers, probably searching for my name.

I clenched my jaw, ready to bolt, but instead offered her an apologetic half-smile. "Sorry. I *am* not. Get that a lot. Based on what I've heard, she's related to me on my father's side…my cousin, I think. Never met her, though."

The lady squeezed my forearm. "The resemblance is striking. If you ever meet her, tell her Deborah is a huge fan."

I forced a curl to my lips. "I will. It was nice meeting you."

"You too, dear."

Before she could add anything else, I hurried to my rental hut, ready for the well-deserved deep tissue massage I'd booked at noon. Riley would go bananas if he knew I'd been spotted just minutes after leaving my room on day one. No doubt he'd have Scooter flown in on a private jet before the day was over.

I shoved that thought aside, my upcoming massage the only thing I cared about for now.

The afternoon passed in a blur. Not feeling like eating dinner at the restaurant and too tired to hit the bar, I ordered room service, swallowed a sleeping pill—those I carried around on tour to defy jet lag—and passed out before the clock even struck ten.

Chapter 3
Gavin

"You've outdone yourself this year, sister," I told Camilla over video call. The grin stretching across her face looked almost Joker-like. "I can't believe you've done this. You know how the holidays are a sensitive subject, yet you sent me to Santa's paradise. Well done. I should've known you'd do something like this one day. Typical Cam."

"Whine as much as you want, Gavin, but you can't stop smiling." She shrugged while trying to hold back her mirth. "The boys and I wanted to help you find your Christmas spirit back. Nothing like being fully immersed in it for two weeks with nowhere to escape. I checked beforehand. There is not much going on outside the resort on this island. So, you see, brother dear, you have no other choice but to embrace the festivities. And get the full experience."

"Cam, most people here are old enough to be either our parents or even our grandparents. You could've at least picked a resort with people my own age. I'm twenty-five in case you didn't remember." I sighed and ran a hand over my face as I crossed the hallway, trying to find a better spot so the wi-fi wouldn't be so spotty.

Camilla's laughter resonated through the line, her face all pixelated on the screen. I paced the lobby of the hotel, trying to find a better signal, worried I might lose the connection.

"Gavin, I'm telling you. By New Year, you'll be a new man. You'll find your spirit back and be ready to move on with your life."

"But—"

"No but. Christmas hasn't cursed you. It's all in your head. Stop being a baby about it and enjoy the rest. You've earned it. You work too much. I'd give anything to lie under the sun right about now. It's snowing here in Michigan, and it's freaking cold. You have no idea how lucky you are."

"You could have come with me," I said with a wink and my most irresistible grin. "Sure you'd like it here. Now let me talk to the boys. I promised them a daily call. Not that I don't like you, sis, but come on, gimme some time to forgive you."

My sister returned my smile, knowing I would never hold a grudge against her.

"Uncle Gavin, Uncle Gavin," Tom said as he stole the phone from his mother. "Are you having fun? Can we see the beach? Is your room like in the pictures Mom showed us? Have you met Santa? Can we come visit you? Will you be back in time for Christmas day?"

I raised a hand to stop his questions, a warm chuckle bubbling out. "Wait a sec, Tom. Too many questions. I haven't met Santa. Not yet, at least. I'm sure he's too busy getting ready for the big night right now. No time to vacation. Christmas is in five days. Let's hope he makes a visit by then. I'll send you pictures of the beach because we'll lose the internet connection if I venture too far from where I am now. And from here you can't see it. I'm sure the pictures won't do justice to this place. It's…it's really something. Never seen anything like this before. What's next?"

I paused, replaying his twenty questions in my head.

"Oh yes. No, you can't come visit because it's a resort only for grown-ups only. So sorry about that. And I won't be home for Christmas morning either. Your mother sent me here, so she'll have to be a good team player and take part in the annual snowball fight with you guys. We'll do a re-match when I come to see you in a few weeks. Anything else?"

"No. I'll think about it and ask more questions tomorrow when we talk. Can you show us around?"

"Sure." I switched the camera so it faced the other direction. Tom gasped at the sight of the giant tree in the middle of the white decor. The lobby had high ceilings and white columns, giving it a Mediterranean vibe. Except for the wall behind the reception desk, it opened to the outside of the resort. The path to the beach, the one to the garden, and a third one to the main road.

"It's all white," my nephew remarked. "Like the snow."

I snickered. "Yep." I pointed to the south side. "The beach is this way. But there is no cell reception down there."

"I hope we go to the beach soon," Tom wished in a dreamy voice. "Bye, Uncle Gavin. Just a second, Matthew wants to talk to you too."

"Bye, big guy. Be nice—"

My little nephew, who had just turned four, grabbed the phone before I could properly say bye to his older brother, and all I could see was his ear. And occasionally, part of his left eyebrow.

"Uncle Gavin, I *lovvve* you."

"I love you too, Matty. What are you doing?"

"Wanna build a snowman, but mommy says I have to wait for the storm to be gone because it's dangerous and I'm too little and the wind will carry me away and I'll have snow in my boots. And I don't like snow in my boots because it's too cold. And when I'm cold, I cry. I'm eating cookies instead."

I hid my grin behind a closed fist.

"Build a snowman in the middle of a storm or eat cookies? Tough choice. I think you made the right one." I lowered my voice. "And for what it's worth, I hate being cold too."

Sherry's voice came through from the background. Camilla's wife was asking my nephew not to wander all around the house with his cookies.

"Uh-oh," Matty whispered like he had been caught with his hand in the jar, his eyes round and his guilty face on, "I need to go."

He spun the phone around, and if I were the kind of person who got dizzy easily, right now would have been my hell. I closed my eyes to keep the room from spinning.

"Okay. We'll talk tomorrow. I love you to Jupiter and back, Matty. Give Tom a kiss for me, would you?"

"Bye, Uncle Gavin. *Lovvve* you too."

He hung up, and with the pad of my thumb, I grazed the screen of my phone. The idea of spending the holidays alone made me jittery. Sure, it wasn't my favorite month of the year, but I liked spending time with my family. Or rather, my sister and her family. That, I would miss.

My stomach rumbled, and I reached the dining hall for a more-than-welcome breakfast. Strangers waved at me, inviting me to join their table, but I wasn't feeling particularly social at that early hour. I offered them a couple of tight-lipped smiles before finding a table by the window, far away from everyone else.

I had flown in yesterday morning, and by now, I'd been asked to enter the sleigh towing, sand snowman building, and cookie decorating contests. The list probably would've kept growing if I'd shown even a hint of excitement. Maybe Camilla was right and I should immerse myself in the experience instead of being miserable for the whole stay. But not before having at least one cup of strong caffeinated beverage, no matter the form. A guy needed caffeine to survive all this craziness.

On day two, I could say the flavored-cream coffee didn't taste as shocking as it did the first time. With my elbows propped on the table, I scanned my surroundings. There were Christmas lights everywhere. Hanging from high ceilings, around the windows, along the bar top, wrapped around palm trees. Anywhere else in the world, it would have looked desperate, but here it kinda fit. Somehow. I couldn't explain it.

The dining hall looked a lot like the resort lobby, except panoramic windows lined the south wall here, giving a glimpse of the pool, a tiki-bar, and a long, unbroken stretch of white sand hugging the edge of the turquoise water of the ocean. From where I sat, I caught sight of some sort of igloo down on the left side of the beach—I still had no idea what it was used for—and wooden reindeers with big red bows around their necks lining the path leading to the resort. Even the *not a big holidays fan* man that I was felt giddy at the magical sight of everything. I had no idea such a place existed on Earth. No doubt people were all happy campers around here. Whatever you did or however you felt, the magic bled on you. For better or for worse. It wouldn't make me enjoy Christmas—nothing could reconcile us—but perhaps it could make the holidays less bitter and more tolerable going forward.

———

The ocean breeze brushed my face, a refreshing contrast to the hot sun baking my skin. I blocked the noises around me, zoning in on the seagulls squawking somewhere behind me and the waves licking the shores. How long was it since I took a well-deserved vacation? I couldn't remember. Right now, I relished the calm washing over me. Camilla was right. I needed this.

"Boy, we need your help. We're one team member short," an old lady called from my left. "My husband hurt his back. We would really need you to take his place."

Nobody answered her.

"Can you hear me?" she asked.

With a deep sigh, I cracked my lids open and slid my sunglasses on the top of my head, looking around, wondering if maybe she was talking to me. She stood two feet from my lounger, dressed in a floral skirt and a Christmas T-shirt, her hands clamped together in front of her in some sort of prayer, her eyes full of expectation.

Was I still asleep, or had I been woken up for another contest I really had no interest in whatsoever?

The sound of waves breaking on the shore caught my attention for a second. With the mid-day sun shining high in the immaculate blue sky, it resembled a field of crystals. Why didn't I go kayaking like I had planned instead of taking a nap on the beach? If I had, I would've escaped this madness for a bit longer.

I blinked, urging my mind to return to the real world, my brain still foggy from the nap.

"Are you in?" the lady asked.

I cocked my head to the side, bringing my attention to her while dragging a hand over my face to wake up my senses. I wasn't going to partake in some silly challenge. Nope. Not this time. Not happening.

I forced an apologetic smile. "Sorry. I don't think so. I'm good right here."

The woman didn't take the hint. Her smile doubled in size, and she closed in on me. "Please. You're a tall man. At five-two, it would come in handy for a woman like me. No matter how hard I try, I can't put the star on top of the tree. That's the most important ornament... The one shining above all others and showing Santa the way. Even perched on my tiptoes, I can't reach the top. And I broke my hip last year, so I can't climb up the stepladder."

I huffed a long breath, lowered my shades back over my eyes, and rubbed my jaw. I squeezed my eyes for a second, wondering which world I had landed in. Jesus, how long had I slept, and what in wild blazes was going on? "Sorry. I can't," I lied.

The anticipation in the lady's eyes faded. Damn it.

One quick look around and I noticed the firs lined up further on the beach and dozens of people around them, sporting cheerful grins.

"Please, son. Help an old lady out."

I pinched my lips together. Why was I even considering this?

I blew out an annoyed breath.

Why couldn't I find it in me to ignore her plea?

"Fine. I'll do it. Just this once, though." I moved to my feet, stretching my arms above my head to shake off the lingering numbness from my nap, fixed my swim shorts which had slipped low, and put my tank top on. The last thing I needed was to have those ladies ask to touch my abs or drool at the sight of a six-pack or make a pass at me. Yeah, it had happened before. Two of my gram's friends at the nursing home when I helped to move furniture around a weekend. One even got all dolled up and asked me out on a date. My friends had a good time roasting me about it for weeks afterward.

"I'm Gavin, by the way."

The old lady tapped my hand. "I'm Ruth. I can't wait to see Dorothea and Callista's faces when they'll see who I recruited to replace Gaston. That's my husband. Fifty-two years and counting," she said, sparks flashing in her fading-green irises. "They won't be able to keep their eyes off you."

I let out a chuckle. Now I'd become a trophy for old women to brag about. I shook my head, my lips curving on their own accord. *Oh, Camilla, you have no idea how sweet the revenge will be,* I said to myself as my smile grew bigger.

"What's the game?" I asked Ruth.

"Decorating a Christmas tree." She squeezed one of my biceps. "And you look strong. All qualities that'll help us win this challenge."

Fuck, what did I get myself into? I hadn't put up a Christmas tree in years.

"*Ho, ho, ho.* Ladies and gentlemen, welcome to our tree decoration contest. You'll have one hour to create the most astonishing fir that will dazzle our guests. The winning team will get to exhibit its work of art in the dining hall. One lucky winner—amongst all the participants—will win a two-hour couples' emmassage voucher at our wellness igloo. Good luck to you all," announced a man in red shorts, a white tee, and a Santa hat through a microphone.

So the igloo turned out to be a massage lodge.

Around us were eight other teams, each made up of four to six people, ready to take on the challenge.

Ruth rubbed her hands together, resembling a kid about to unwrap the biggest gift under the tree. Okay, perhaps I could put my broodiness away for an hour and be a team player.

"Listen, team," she said, "this is Mr. Gavin, and he will help us. He's tall and sturdy like the tree we are going to decorate." She cupped her mouth, then whispered to her elderly friends. "Have you seen those arms? They look good enough to bite. Don't look, but I can tell big-mouth Dorothea and catty Callista are watching us….huh, watching him. Let's give them a run for their money."

They all giggled as I huffed and rolled my eyes. I could feel my ears reddening from embarrassment. Did I travel back in time to my high school years? I turned around and faced my teammates. They all gave me once-overs and innocent stares. Well, ladies, have a look then. Just for show, I flexed my left biceps, and the giggles multiplied. I sighed. This would be fun. Well, maybe fun wasn't the right term. Let's say interesting. Yeah, that sounded better.

Ruth nudged my arm. "Mr. Gavin, these are my friends, Tea and Dolly. And there's my husband, Gaston," she introduced, indicating a man dressed in a reindeer-patterned shirt sitting on a lounger. I waved at the man who returned it. "Mr. Gavin will do all the heavy lifting and take care of the treetop. And also, he'll distract the other teams because he's handsome and smells great." Damn it, I was being objectified by a group of old ladies. "Tea, you do the lighting, and Dolly and I will build garlands with seashells because we're the ones with the best eyesight between us three."

All the women nodded. If they had attended high school together, no doubt Ruth would have been the leader. The captain of the cheerleading squad. Or the class president. She had that natural leadership quality.

"*Ho, ho, ho.* Ready, set, go," the man with the microphone said as he rang a bell, signaling the contest had begun. "You have one hour. Show us your best creation."

For the next sixty minutes, we built a Christmas tree on a white sand beach in the middle of the Caribbean Sea. How had my life come down to this?

When the bell rang after the hour was up, we stepped back to admire our work.

"It's beautiful," Tea said on my right, squeezing my hand. "You did a great job with the top, Mr. Gavin. Thank you for helping us out."

I returned her contagious grin.

These ladies had grown on me in the last hour, and they had even invited me to their Christmas Eve celebrations later this week.

Once again, I didn't have the energy to refuse or make excuses to avoid them. I had nothing better to do anyway, and no plans—except spending the night in my room, on my own, watching movies like I often did back home. Since here they only showed Christmas movies on TV—and I usually watched action or thrillers—having a group of friends didn't sound so bad.

The man dressed in an islander's version of Santa spoke. "All day people will vote for their favorite tree. The winning team will be announced tonight at dinner. But for now, let's do the raffle draw." A clumsy beat, like a drumroll, tumbled from his lips. "And the winner is…Gavin Moore."

Ruth pushed me forward. "It's you, Mr. Gavin. You won. You won!" she cheered, clapping her hands.

Fantastic. What would I do with a couple's massage?

Chapter 4

Aisha

The music started, and the dancers filled the stage. A man, over six feet tall with muscular arms and defined washboard abs—enough to make an old lady lose her dentures—lifted me high in his arms, and sitting on his broad shoulder, his hand hooked to my thigh, I sang my new top-charter. An upbeat country song with a chorus so catchy it was almost impossible to get it out of your head once you heard it. Dressed in a sequined silver tiered mini and high-heeled flashy-pink cowboy boots with fringes and glitter, I shone onstage.

Aisha Jones—aka me—was the leading name in pop country. I'd climbed the charts fast and steady for the last seven years. When I was a little girl, I used to sing pop songs on a children's TV show. Then, in my teen years, I'd joined an all-girl group for two years before shifting to a solo career, focusing on the style of music I truly loved. Growing up in Nashville, country music had always been one of my favorites. Now, at twenty-six, I mixed both country and pop and had an impressive fan base all around the world.

Muscle Man lowered me to the ground and spun me around. I arched my back and stared at the ceiling, rainwater falling from above as I sang and danced, my clothes soaked, water splashing every time I stomped my feet.

The crowd erupted in cheers.

My body froze, but not from the cold. Something didn't feel right. I frowned, trying to peer into the darkness that soon enveloped me. Where was all this water coming from? Was this a dream?

I peeled my heavy lids open to a *tss-tss* sound and some kind of deafening alarm. I jolted from flat on my back to sitting at ninety degrees in a heartbeat, my thoughts still fuzzy from sleep.

Sitting at the edge of the bed, I yawned, trying to separate reality from the dream.

Where was I? And why was someone hosing me down in the middle of the night?

My brain worked hard to process the situation. It didn't help that I couldn't see a thing in this total blackness.

Hotel. Vacation. Island. Sleeping pill.

It all came back to me.

Using my hand as a visor to prevent water from blinding me, I tried to recoup my thoughts.

My head throbbed, jets of water hitting it from every angle.

I remembered the lamp on the bedside table within arm's reach and stretched out my hand to turn it on, needing some light to assess the damage. And the flood. It flashed when I turned the knob—a short-circuit electric jolt that lit up the room in a sizzling blue glow, frying the lamp. Great. Water and electricity hated each other. How did I forget?

For how long had I been passed out in the rain? How could I not have woken up sooner? Anger seared inside me. My nose tingled. That musty smell…was it like muddy water? It had a way of penetrating my sensitive nose like an unwelcome guest and clinging to my nostrils.

I threaded my way across the flooded floor, arms stretched out before me to avoid bumping into anything, each step a struggle against an ocean current, with more water pouring down over me. If I owned a canoe, no doubt I'd be able to paddle across my room right now as the level reached well above my ankles. Where was all this rain coming from? Was a tropical storm ravaging outside? A dozen steps later, my hands encountered a sturdy surface —the wall—and I backed against it, using the alcove to shelter me from the ongoing shower.

My brain finally computed, and I recalled plugging my phone next to the high-end espresso machine, somewhere on my right, before going to bed. With one hand, I tapped around until my fingers connected with my precious device. I huffed a long breath. Small victory.

With a shaky finger, I turned the flashlight mode on.

My heart sank in my chest, and I wanted to howl in frustration at the sight before me. Hot moisture dampened my eyes.

Water dripped from the ceiling in mighty jets.

The entire room was completely soaked, including my stuff. The white fluffy bed linen had turned a dull shade of gray. My beloved room had become one from a horror movie. I feared I would throw up as surges of acid swirled inside me, but I didn't need to add to the pungent odor that was surrounding me. The moldy smell had taken over my olfactory senses, and I fought off the waves of nausea threatening my stomach.

I drew deep breaths to calm the turmoil seething inside me.

The water continued spraying the room and now reached about a foot in height, much higher than I imagined at first. No wonder I thought I could wade through the tide a few minutes ago. Black watery streaks lined the immaculate white walls.

This was a disaster.

I raised my eyes and realized that the water was coming from the heads of the fire sprinklers.

Stagnant water. Ugh. God forbid should something happen to me from the water in those pipes. At least now I knew where that gray, stomach-churning rain came from.

Tears ran down my face, mixing with the smelly deluge that almost drowned me in my sleep. With my fingers, I wiped my cheeks.

How could this happen to me?

My shoulders sagged in defeat, and I sighed. Something deep inside me splintered. All I'd wished for was a two-week vacation in paradise. Sun. Beach. Palm trees. More hot tears streamed down my cheeks. At that moment, it hit me. Ohmygod. What would I do now?

Amid everything, I hadn't heard the pounding on the door. After I sniffled my sadness away, I opened the door using my phone to guide me only to find George standing on the other side, ready to knock again, his hand still in mid-action, floating in front of his chest, a flashlight in the other.

"Oh, Ms. Jones. You awake," he said in his thick Spanish accent. "Here to get you. You need to evacuate. Leave. Leave now."

I looked over my shoulder. "What about my stuff?" It

was stupid. Why bother, right? Everything must have been ruined by now anyway.

"You get it tomorrow. When daylight. Now too dark. And the pump won't turn off."

"The pump?"

"Fire sprinklers," George explained.

"Oh. There's a fire? Does the entire resort have to evacuate?"

George's lips twitched into a disheartened downward tilt. "No, Ms. Jones," he said through a heavy sigh. "The man next door hung Christmas lights to sprinkler heads. System went off. No fire."

I nodded because I had nothing to say that could make any of this better. Instead, I tightened my grip around my phone, the only thing I'd rescued from my wrecked room.

We reached the pool area, and George fished a towel out. I took it with sagging shoulders, wishing it had been a pair of flip-flops instead. Priorities. Drenched from head to toes, it would take more than a towel to dry myself up. With trembling fingers, I wrapped the piece of terry cloth around me, unable to refuse the man while he watched me with a wary expression.

"Good. Ms. Jones, you will be going to another hotel. Bed and dry clothes. Go to the shuttle."

My heels dug into the ground. I stopped in my tracks and grabbed his forearm, forcing him to look at me.

"No. *No, no, no.* Ms. Jones not going away to another hotel. Ms. Jones staying here. Can't you find a room in this hotel until mine gets fixed?"

"No. Hotel is full. Holidays. Found a room for you at Las Palmeras. You'll love it there. Festive and fun. Great hotel."

Las Palmeras? It didn't sound so bad.

Palm trees. Sun. Beach. Maybe it could work.

"Fine. Only for a night, okay?"

George tapped my hand still clutching his forearm. "We'll see, Ms. Jones. We'll see."

Thirty minutes later, I was stuffed in that thing resembling a shuttle with the air conditioner blowing icy cold air, freezing me through my soaking wet clothes, surrounded by four people. For a reason I couldn't explain, I had gone to bed in sweatpants and a T-shirt last night whereas I usually slept in only panties. Thank God I had the decency to put them on after my jaunt at the beach yesterday. The sleeping pill had acted fast, and I had passed out before undressing completely.

The old lady beside me cried in her husband's arms.

Another woman—her fiery eyes were like weapons about to slay the man sitting beside her—waggled a finger at him, cursing in Spanish. Was he the one who thought hanging stupid shit from a sprinkler head was the idea of the century? By the look of the woman, whom I assumed to be the wife, I concluded a big fat juicy *Yes*.

With a dramatic roll of my eyes, I leaned my head back and closed my lids, the vibration of the small bus making me sleepy. That damn pill would take hours to get out of my system.

After what seemed like seconds, the sobbing lady patted my arm. "Miss, we're here."

Blinking to get my brain to reboot, I mirrored her smile and rose to my feet to exit the bus. "Gracias," I told the driver.

The moment my feet touched the last step, my heart entangled in itself. I was pretty sure I'd have a heart attack. This was a joke. Someone was playing a prank on me. Or karma was a bitch. Either way, now wasn't the time to mess with me. All I craved was a hot shower and a comfy bed.

And all I got was this.

I blinked again. And rubbed my eyes with my fists. I blinked once more. No, it wasn't a vision. Or a dream. Damn it, could it be real?

Perhaps I was still asleep? That must be it. My sleeping pill could do that to me, right? Induce nightmares. The kind that sent chills to your neck because they seemed so real.

With a hand over my pounding organ, I forced some oxygen in.

My perfect vacation just took a turn for the worse.

I traced the sign of the cross with my hand. Whoa, I hadn't done one of those in forever. Right now, though, I'd do about anything to escape the night.

Chapter 5

Aisha

Christmas Wonderland. Written in big glittery letters, lit up by a projector below. Even through the darkness, I couldn't miss it. They made sure of it. In the lobby, I couldn't miss noticing a giant twenty-foot-tall Christmas tree, garlands, lights—too many lights—and an inflatable giant snowman. My stomach churned. Bile seared the back of my throat. A red train pulling three wagons was parked right by the lobby archway, with a wooden "North Pole Express" sign next to it. Shaking my head fast, as if I could unsee the sight, I stepped back into the vehicle.

"Sorry," I told the driver, "not going in there. *No, no, no.* Allergic to Christmas. Not happening."

"Don't like Christmas? Everybody does," he said, his accent thicker than George, a disapproving frown creasing the dark skin of his forehead. "Need to go. Can't sleep in bus."

"There must be another hotel around. Drive me somewhere else. *Pleaaase.*"

"No other hotel. All full. Holidays. Lots of tourists. Miss needs to stay here."

With his chin, he pointed me in the direction of what I could only define as my personal hell. Lucifer's sanctuary. The netherworld.

"Can I stay at your place? I'll pay you. I can—"

"Sorry, Miss. No room. Too small. Miss must stay here. With other people. Now go."

Every swear word I knew spewed out of my mouth as I stepped out. My heart leaped to my throat and lodged there. Panic fluttered its tiny wings in my chest. Through slit eyes, I observed the scene playing out all around me. Could I run somewhere? Seek refuge elsewhere? Find a nice family to lodge with? In the middle of the night on an island. Yeah, not happening. My chest deflated, and my dreams and hopes for this vacation sank. Drowned. Died. No. They couldn't be settled to this…that…this finality, could they?

I would turn this around, reclaim my precious vacation in paradise, get my momentum back. Yes, I'd find a way to fix this. A yawn broke my train of thoughts. But tomorrow. After I got up. Right now, only a hot shower could make up for this thing…this…this nightmare I found myself in.

"Let's do this," I said to myself. "Keep your head down… It's just for a night, okay? *You can do this. You have to.* Think about the hot shower, the dry clothes, a warm meal." Yeah, I could do this. One night surrounded by everything Christmassy wouldn't kill me. It would just make me appreciate my perfect hotel even more later.

If this wouldn't kill me, then it would make me stronger. Wasn't that how the saying went? Time to find out. And to prove it to myself.

With a stiff back and a newfound determination, I entered the lobby, immediately being greeted by employees wearing Santa hats or reindeer headbands with flashing antlers. *Just for a night*, I reminded myself. *One night. One night. One night.*

Better make this my new mantra. Or turn it into a new song. No. No Christmas song.

In a room decorated with a red plushy bedspread and a shower curtain showing Mrs. Claus baking cookies—I sucked in a deep breath when my eyes landed on it—I removed my wet clothes. *One night. One night. One night.* After a long, hot shower that drained some of the tension away from my back and upper neck, I put on the hotel-branded striped red and white bathrobe. Why was everything here Christmassy? I had to give it to Las Palmeras because they had that thematic thing going on strong. Most marketing firms should take notes.

At almost four in the morning, I finally laid my head on a pillow, and it took mere minutes before sleep claimed me again as I said a silent prayer, hoping this was all a dream after all and I'd wake up in the morning and none of this would be real.

———

The knock on the door woke me up from my deep slumber. I had the most awful dream last night. Today was a new day, and I could forget all about it. A smile peeked on my lips as the sun beamed through my closed lids. Did I forget to close the curtains before going to bed? "Good morning, Playa De La Isla Azul," I greeted the day as I pried my eyes open, smiling wide.

The curve of my lips flattened the more I glanced around. Red bedspread. A Christmas tree in the corner by the window. Candy cane curtains with a white garland hem. Multicolor lights hanging over the bed. And here I thought I had dreamed the entire night. Sprinklers, shuttle ride, giant Christmas tree, North Pole Express. It all came back to me in a violent surge.

"No. Please, no." It had really happened. All of it. Oh man. My airway clamped shut, trapping the air inside. I blinked a million times, cupping my throbbing heart with both hands. Was this how heart failure felt?

Last night wasn't a nightmare. It was real life...*my* life. I blinked again. For good measure. It did nothing. Everything stayed the same. The last traces of my smile dissolved. My composure shattered, leaving my chest hollow. I dragged a hand over my face. Nothing I did erased the horrifying vision surrounding me.

Oh god, I had slept in Santa Land.

Anxiety coiled in my stomach.

"Why?" I asked out loud, my voice high-pitched. "What did I do to deserve this?" My eyes brimmed with hot tears. "Please, someone help me out of this. I'm begging you. If you can hear me, pull me out of here."

Whoever decorated this room was either blind or had a sick sense of humor.

Knock. Knock. Knock.

Oh yes, the door. I shut my eyes for a second, calming the storm stirring deep inside me. Coffee. I needed coffee. Strong. With a dash of cream. And a reality check. Fast.

On my feet, I pounded to the door and yanked it open. Maybe my savior was standing on the other side. Someone rescuing me and bringing me back to my paradise resort, swearing this whole night was a mistake.

"*Ho, ho, ho.* Good morning, Ms. Jones," the woman— Stella, according to her name tag—said, a large grin brightening her face, her dark hair loose over her shoulders, wearing a Santa hat and elves shoes.

This sick joke had lasted long enough.

Everything inside me screamed, but I pasted my best poker face on, fighting the grimace waiting to take over my mouth. Instead, I inhaled for a long second and faked being happy to see her. "Morning. Nice shoes."

A light flush spread across Stella's cheeks when she thanked me.

The woman held out her arms, offering me a pile of clothes.

"For you. From the hotel lobby store. According to the size you mentioned on the form you filled last night after you arrived. See what fits." She placed the flip-flops hanging from her fingers on top. "Size eight. As requested."

At least they were plain white without any embellishments or anything Christmas-like.

"Oh, and a toiletry kit. Along with a cap and shades."

I looked at her in askance.

"In case you wanna go," she whispered, glancing around as if we were being watched, "incognito."

I blew out a breath. Finally, someone with common sense around here. "Thank you," I said. "Please tell me. Where can I get coffee?"

"Dining hall. We're serving pancakes this morning. You should hurry, They're pretty popular. Better get down there soon, or there won't be any left."

"Thanks. After the night I had, pancakes sound amazing."

Carbs and coffee. Yes, I needed those right now.

"Have a great day, Ms. Jones. And call me if you need anything."

Yes. A new hotel room. No, my previous hotel room. And all my stuff.

Once Stella left, I hurried inside my room and kicked the door shut.

Starving, I let the bathrobe fall to the floor and I rummaged through the clothes Stella brought me.

"*Nooo.* Why? Who ordered this torture on me?" I yelled with my arms raised as if whoever up there had thought this joke to be funny could hear my plea and fix this.

Okay, this was some test…some prank. It had to be. Was Riley behind this? To teach me a lesson for refusing to perform at the New Year's Eve concert? No way the people at this resort could be serious. Every piece of clothing either had reindeers or snowmen or Santa's face on them. Did I land in another dimension last night? Did a door open in the sky and teleport me somewhere other than Earth?

My thoughts swirled in my head, and I buried my face in my hands, emotions threatening to spill over.

The urge to call Stella back and ask her to get me non-Christmas clothes in exchange for a big tip sounded like the best idea right about now, but no doubt it would be seen as insensitive and rude. And to add insult to injury, she knew who I was… or at least knew of me. I was clearly out of luck.

With a fresh batch of tears clouding my vision, I dropped on the bed, ready to forfeit.

The next plane out of here was scheduled at the end of the week. I knew because I had checked last night after I got here.

I grabbed my phone, ready to text my manager so he could save me—and he would, I knew he would—but after I typed "SOS," my fingers halted, floating over the screen.

This was a bad idea. What if Riley asked me to

perform in New York in exchange for bringing me back home? I'd never be able to refuse him after he saved me from this nightmare. And I'd never hear the end of it.

All my important stuff, passport and purse included, was locked in the safe at Domingo Resort. Unless I could get them, I was bound to dress like Santa's help for now. I was used to people doing the impossible to please me, but this time, my options were very limited…if not entirely absent.

You can do this, I reminded myself. *One night. Or rather one day. A few hours at the most, and you'll get your dream vacation back.*

My stomach grumbled on point, to tell me to hurry. Oh yes, the pancake breakfast. No way was I also missing breakfast. My bad luck had to run out at some point. Swallowing down my dislike, I tried a few pieces of clothing and ended up wearing a white knee-length summer halter dress that fit kinda nicely if you forgot about the candy canes pattern that covered it.

As I finished getting ready, braiding my now crazy mess of curly hair, thanks to last night's downpour and lack of a flat iron, I avoided looking at my reflection in the mirror, not ready to assess the extent of the damages. I didn't even have my precious lipstick with me. The one that made me feel powerful and brave whenever I applied it.

With my new shades on, I reached the lobby, looking for the dining hall—or a way out of this. Nah, this could wait. Food first. Escape plan later.

My legs refused to move forward when I entered the dining area. Stomach-churning, eye-burning sight. Something I wished could be erased from my memory. Forever. I had to fight the temptation to plug my ears with my fingers and stare at the floor. Christmas music played from every speaker—no fewer than dozens of them. Everyone was dressed in silly Christmas-themed clothes.

Once my feet agreed to keep moving, a man with dark skin and darker hair, wearing a Santa apron, greeted me before I could flee. "*Ho, ho, ho.* Good morning. Hungry?"

I narrowed my eyes. And bit back a cry. Enough with the "*Ho, ho, ho.*" What happened to "*hola*"?

"Starving," I mumbled, keeping my gaze down to avoid all the overbearing decorations in my line of vision and pushing down the murderous thoughts filling my brain.

"Follow me." The man led me to a table near a large window, giving me a great view of the donut-shaped resort pool, a bar in the middle, and the white sand beach with the azure ocean just beyond.

As if he had a direct line to my stomach—and my thoughts—the server came back with a cup of coffee and a pitcher of cream seconds later.

"Thank you," I said, letting the comforting odor fill my nostrils and pouring some cream into my liquid caffeine. At least the god who sent me here had some decency left.

With the mug nestled between my hands, I brought the hot divinity to my lips. In just two seconds—three at most—I spat my drink all over the square table. "What the fuck is that?" I asked out loud, mostly to myself, wiping the drops dripping from my lips with the back of my hand.

A loud baritone chuckle resonated next to me. A man, handsome, with tousled dark hair, a mischievous smile hot enough to melt Antarctica, and enticing sky-blue eyes watched me.

"That would be peppermint cream. It can be surprising the first time you try it. It's my third morning, and it's slowly growing on me. You'll get used to it in no time. You'll even miss it once you go back home. I'm confident."

"Impossible. This is disgusting. What's wrong with

everyone here? Why can't I have a normal vacation? And what's with the omnipresent holiday vibe?"

The man moved to his feet and wiped the corner of my mouth with a napkin. Tiny spurs of electricity shot through me. Sensations, until now, I never knew existed. "Sorry," he said, "you had some cream there."

He smirked. Our eyes locked on each other, and at that instant, I forgot everything I wanted to whine about. Until he sat down in his chair.

"You're not a big Christmas fan, are you?"

I sighed. "The truth?"

He nodded.

"It may hurt you," I said, scrunching up my nose. "I hate Christmas. All of it. It's some commercial holiday that pushes people to spend a huge amount of money just to prove to their friends and family they're important. There are much better ways to show your loved ones you care about them."

"Oh, you're one of those, aren't you?" he stated with thick furrowed brows, the smirk illuminating his face, perfect in every way. I arched my eyebrows, waiting for him to explain. "You know, the one who thinks Christmas is a cliché?" Chin dimple. Pearly white teeth. Full lips.

I shrugged. "Guess I am. Doesn't make me a bad person, though."

"Never said that. One question, though. Why did you book a room at Las Palmeras if you hate Christmas? It's a year-long holiday-themed resort."

I coughed. Life was messing with me. I had no more doubts. Stupid karma.

"Geez. It explains so much. I didn't know. Had a room at Domingo Resort, but Santa peed on me and sent me to hell."

The man frowned. "Santa? You sure? Seems very unlikely of him."

He offered me a crooked smile, looking irresistible. Why did he have to be so good-looking? It messed with my thoughts. Even fully clothed, he looked fit. His golden skin, the color of freshly baked cinnamon rolls, thanks to the tan he wore, would probably compare to velvet under the pads of my fingers if he let me caress him. Whoa, enough dirty thoughts. His lips twitched, and I catapulted myself out of his magnetic field.

"Maybe not Santa, but for some reason, I believe he has something to do with this. Like he wants to teach me a lesson or mess with me. Who knows? Who else could be behind this?" I asked, waving a hand around. "Unless it's karma's fault… Anyway, some smart dude hung Christmas lights from the sprinkler head in the pavilion next to mine. We were connected to the same emergency line. I'm sure you can figure out the rest."

A whispered *Oh* left his gorgeous lips. *Gorgeous, huh? Really, girl?*

"Anyway, it resembled a flooded war zone when I left in the middle of the night. I woke up drenched. They had no vacant room and sent me here for a day until the mess is taken care of."

The man burst out laughing, and for a second, I wasn't sure if I should be offended or just go along with it.

"What's so funny?"

"If the damages are as bad as you describe them, there's no way you'll be back in your room within the next month. Fixing a fire sprinkler system isn't a job you can do in just a few hours. We're on an island. I'm sure they have to order their supplies from the mainland." And he started laughing again.

My breath caught in my throat. There was no way he

was telling the truth. "You're kidding, right? You're making fun of me," I accused, crossing my arms over my chest.

"I wish. Sorry to be the one bearing the bad news. Seems like you're about to spend your vacation dressed in elf clothes, drinking peppermint-flavored coffee, dancing to Christmas carols. I'm sure you'll look pretty with reindeer antlers on. Should I get you a headband?" The back of my eyeballs burned, but I couldn't decide if it was from fury or tears. The man's amusement faded. "For what it's worth, I'm not a big Christmas fan either."

"Why are you here then? Being a bit sadomasochist? Enjoying the pain?"

"Not really. I love my lovemaking without gag balls and whips. Those are overrated anyway." He winked, and I hesitated between wanting to kiss that smirk off his lips or partaking in his game. "My sister. She sent me here. A gift from her and her family. An inside joke between us. Anyway, it's better being here than sad and lonely back home. At least people are cheerful here. I hope it'll bleed on me… eventually." He raked his fingers through his dark locks, messing it up, my own fingers itching to comb them back into place. "You should definitely add Christmas clothes to your wardrobe. They suit you… And make your eyes pop."

I poked my tongue out. "Real funny. Wait until I put a Santa hat on. You'll be bewildered. Red is *so* my color."

The server brought a stack of red pancakes sprinkled with white and green sugary cut-outs in front of me—as if the natural color of food were banned—and I dug in, starving.

Beside me, the annoying yet handsome man with sinful lips and mesmerizing eyes extended his hand. "I'm Gavin, by the way. Gavin Moore."

After wiping mine on a napkin, I returned his handshake, the feel of his warm palm in mine sending my heart into overdrive. "Aisha. Aisha Jones." I grimaced. Why did I use my real name? I usually came up with a fake identity around strangers.

Gavin tsk-tsked. "I knew it was you. I was about to remark you look just like her. Saw you at a concert once. With Carter Hills and Sam Stevens. And a bunch of other folks. A festival. In Texas." He studied me for a moment. "Listen, I won't tell anyone," he said. "For what it's worth, your identity is safe with me. From what I've seen, you attract a crazy number of fans… And some are actually crazy for real. How do you manage?"

"*Igivethemfake*," I mumbled under my breath.

"What? What did you say?"

I sighed. "I pretend to be my cousin or a doppelgänger and give them a fake name."

Gavin let out a huge roar of laughter that caused heads to turn."Is that so? Done. From now on, I'll call you Maggie. It fits you. Yeah, you'll be Maggie to me."

A smile spread across my face. Nothing I did could contain it. This man had a way to cheer me up. To make me forget about all the things bothering me.

"Maggie's fine. Let's start over." I held out my hand. "Hi, I'm Maggie."

"Gavin. Nice to meet you." His palm released mine, leaving tingly sensations behind. Gavin rose to his feet. "Maybe we'll see each other again, Maggie. I need to call my nephews, I promised I'd call them every morning. Have a nice one."

The man weaved between the tables and disappeared toward the lobby. My eyes lingered on his backside. Long, muscled legs, firm ass, well-defined back tapering into a narrow waist—I had a weakness for toned trapezius muscles—and brown hair that I wanted to mess up even more.

Blanking out the hum of conversations around me and with no one disturbing me, I was left alone with a new wave of murderous thoughts, with just my red pancakes, wretched coffee, and hair-ripping music for company.

I rolled my shoulders back and puffed my chest out. No way I'd stay here and do nothing about it. I was Aisha Jones. I had resources. Time to get myself sprung out of this nightmare.

With purpose in my step, I reached the lobby, about to plead—or buy—my way out of here, but then my eyes landed on a tall figure.

Dark hair. Blue eyes. Sexy body.

Heat spread inside me.

To hell with my newfound mission.

Maybe I could survive this place for another day?

Chapter 6
Gavin

"**D**id you make friends? What are their names? Are you having fun? We built a gingerbread house last night. And the biggest snowman. And snow angels. And ran around with Middle," Middle being the dog. The middle child as Camilla often said.

My nephews' eyes shone through the screen. I loved these video chat sessions with them. Back home, we had them a few times a week since we lived in different states. It'd become a part of our routine. This way I didn't miss out on Tom and Matthew growing up.

The boys laughed when I raised a finger, knowing what it meant. "Lots of friends here." I scratched my forehead to add some effect. "So many of them, I can't remember their names. Send me a picture of the gingerbread house so I can see what I'm missing. Snow angels and a giant snowman, are you two messing with me? I can't believe I missed that." I facepalmed, and they giggled. "You're lucky

I'm stuck here for two weeks, or I would have jumped on the first plane to Michigan."

We talked some more and hung up. I sighed. Christmas was in three days. I had no clue how I'd go through this day on my own.

After hitting the gym and showering, I changed into swim trunks and an unbuttoned shirt covered in palm trees, and headed to the beach. Ruth and Gaston waved at me and motioned for me to join them, their smiles wide enough to encompass the entire Christmas cheer of the resort.

"Hey, how you guys doing?" I asked, shaking my head when Ruth asked me to sit down. "I'm waiting for someone. I need to get going soon." Nobody was waiting for me, but I didn't feel like hanging out with a group of chatty women feeding on gossip right now.

Ruth stood up and squeezed my forearm. "It's okay, dear. Did you make friends? You look like a lonely man. It will be good for you to enjoy some company." We shared tight-lipped smiles. "But you're welcome to hang out with us anytime. Gaston is always happy to have some male company because he keeps complaining the girls and I talk too much."

"Yes, they do," Gaston retorted, bobbing his head.

I returned his smile and winked. "Thank you. I—" Aisha stepped into my line of sight, strolling on the beach all alone, her arms wrapped around herself. She was wearing that striking candy-cane dress that hugged her figure, drawing my eyes to her curves. "Actually, huh…my friend is here. I need to go." I turned on my heel and watched the elderly couple over my shoulder as I sauntered away. "Thank you for the offer. We'll catch up later."

"That's your friend?" Ruth asked. "She's pretty." She

made a swooshing motion with her hand. "Go now. Don't make her wait."

"Hey, Maggie," I called out, running after her, "wait up."

Aisha turned around as I closed the distance between us. God, I forgot how gorgeous she was.

"Okay, could you pretend to be really happy to see me for a second? I have friends over there," I said, pointing with my thumb in the direction of Ruth and Gaston, "who are chatterboxes and big on rumors. I'm trying to get away." I winced. "Could use your help right about now."

Aisha offered me a pointed look, her hip tipped to one side, arms folded over her chest, pushing her tits up. My gaze dropped to the swell of her breast before moving back up to her eyes. "You? All tall and muscular, need my help to escape people old enough to be your grandparents? Are you bullshitting me, Gavin?"

I shook my head and stuffed my hands in my pockets, glancing down as a ghost of a curl grazed my lips.

"Well…when you say it like this, it sounds..huh…bad?" I lifted my eyes to meet hers. "Still, could you pretend to be my friend for a bit, so they'll let me be this afternoon?" I wiggled an eyebrow, and Aisha let out a laugh so warm, it infused my body with waves of heat. "If not, they'll rope me into some Christmas challenge or another, and I'm really not feeling the spirit today." I dragged a hand over my face. "And I'm the worst at turning them down."

Without a warning and with a grin plastered on, Aisha snaked her arm through mine and pulled me forward. With just a touch, she sent my heartbeat into a frenzy. "Come on, friend, walk with me. I could use the company."

We moved side by side in silence while I kicked pieces

of shell with my big toe. "Any news about the flood at your non-Christmas hotel?"

She sighed, looking in the distance, the tide washing her feet.

"Nah. They told me my stuff has been sent to the cleaner. I don't know… I'll be able to access the safe tomorrow, so my passport and other valuables are good."

"How long are you stuck in Christmas land with us?" From the side, I noticed her shoulders tensing. "Hey, it's okay."

Aisha turned, and her dark eyes brimmed with tears. Our gazes locked, and after a long second, she buried her face in her hands. "This vacation is supposed to be amazing… Not spent in a hotel in Mistletoe Heaven, drinking disgusting-flavored coffee, dressed as Santa's elf," she cried out, tugging at her dress. "I'd packed that glittery red dress along with other amazing outfits for this vacation, to feel beautiful. And sexy. And good about myself… I wasn't supposed to worry about all the Christmas stuff for two weeks. It's silly… I know." Her shoulders sagged forward. "I'm sorry. I'm not always complaining. I swear."

My fingers itched to brush away the wild tendrils of her hair sticking to her cheeks, thanks to the salty breeze. For a long second, I watched her. "It's not complaining when you planned something and it all went to shit."

"I sound superficial. It's just…" She took a sharp breath. "I went to the front desk. Since I don't have my passport, I can't leave. Anyway, where would I go? I booked this vacation almost a year ago. I refuse to go home, and every resort is seemingly full at this time of the year… That's what they told me. It's not like I have a choice."

Aisha looked defeated. A fat tear rolled down her cheek, and I caught it before it reached her chin. We both froze, the pad of my thumb still on her skin. Transfixed by her beauty—and her vulnerability—I studied the pattern of her manicured dark eyebrows, black irises, straight nose, and full mouth. Having her so close sent a zing straight to my groin.

Every part of me became attuned to her.

Aisha's breathing picked up, and I blinked away the magnetic hold she had on me.

"I have an idea." A thought flashed through my head, and I grabbed her hand. The contact of our skin quieted the unfamiliar angst stirring inside me. That made no sense. No doubt, my hyperactive imagination was to blame. Aisha eyed me, waiting for me to explain myself. "Follow me."

"Where?" she asked, without taking a step forward.

"You'll see."

Hand in hand, as if we'd done this a thousand times before, we reached the resort and crossed the hotel lobby. After the guy at the front desk gave me instructions, I knew where to go and led her toward the shuttle stop.

"Gavin, where are you taking me?" she asked. "I'm not in the mood to parade through town dressed like I came straight from the North Pole. I would hate to end up on the front page of a magazine looking like this."

"Maggie, be a good sport. This dress looks good on you. I swear. It's just a silly pattern, nothing to make a big deal about. Trust me, okay? You'll thank me later."

A shuttle ride and fifteen minutes later, we arrived on a small street—a place where locals lived, not meant for tourists. The man at the front desk told me I'd see a blue water tower once we reached our destination. Holding the map he'd drawn for me on a scrap of paper, I followed his instructions.

We slipped into a quiet little shop through a narrow

alley paved with white cobblestones and lined with palm trees. Soft salsa music played from the ajar door. The entire time, I kept my hand resting on her lower back. "Are we trespassing?" she asked, her eyes widening. This vulnerable look suited her. It made her seem like a mere mortal, not a superstar.

I peeked inside, assaulted by the colorful display before me. Yes, we were at the right place. "Get wild," I exclaimed, moving my arm to let Aisha in first.

"Wait. What? How? You've taken me shopping?" she asked, rubbing a pink velvety fabric between her fingers. "Gavin, this is the nicest thing someone has done for me in a while." She turned around, a disarming smile illuminating her face.

"What are you waiting for? Get crazy and pick everything you need. I have nowhere else to be, so take your time."

As if we were in a movie scene, she tried on two dozen different outfits, giving me a peek at each one and asking for my opinion—like it actually mattered to her.

On a plush chair, I watched her, grinning like a fool. I hadn't had this much fun in a long time. Simple. And addictive.

A breezy yellow-and-white striped shirt? "No."

A white maxi dress contrasting with her dark skin? "Oh yes."

A golden and black skirt: "You should get two of those."

A tiny black bikini: "Yes, please."

On her tiptoes, she pressed her lips to my cheek after finding a few outfits she liked. My whole body reacted to her closeness. Again.

"What's that for?"

The genuine happiness in her smile sent a rush of warmth through me. "For doing all this."

After checking out, Aisha disappeared into a dressing room to put on the white maxi that made her look like royalty. Behind a cream linen curtain, a splash of colorful fabric caught my eye. The lady on the other side, in her late fifties, greeted me with a smile as I pointed to something.

———

"No, I can't let you pay for dinner," Aisha said, shaking her phone, reminding me she could use it to pay the bill. It turned out to be useful earlier at the store since her wallet was still trapped in the safe in her room at Domingo Resort.

"I insist," I said, catching the waiter's attention when I waved my card. "Anyway, it would be considered rude here to let a lady pay for her meal." I shrugged. "Sometimes those nineteen-fifties rules are still appealing."

Aisha shook her head. "If you say so. Guess we'll need to go out again so I can return the favor."

I flashed her a large grin. "Anytime you want, woman."

After dinner, we strolled on the beach under the moonlight, neither of us ready to go back to the hotel. "I love it here," Aisha said. "It's peaceful."

"Oh, you mean you love that there's no Christmas display anywhere around here. I can't believe a good-looking tree and some sugary treats don't entice you."

She elbowed my side. "Why are you here, Gavin? By yourself? What happened to you?"

"I could ask you the same question."

She pressed my forearm with her small hand, and my body tensed, then relaxed, under her touch.

We sat on a large rock overlooking the dark ocean, only lit up by the full moon mirroring on its surface.

"My sister thought it would help me find my Christmas spirit back."

"You lost it, or you never had one to begin with?"

I huffed. "I don't know. It's been so long… Growing up, every bad thing in my life happened around this day. I broke my wrist at five. My mom lost her job the week before Christmas when I was seven. My cat, Sneezy, died on Christmas Eve when I was eleven. My grandpa had a heart attack two days after Christmas when I was nineteen. In college, someone broke into my apartment during the holiday vacation.

"As a kid, I wrote to Santa and begged him for a happy Christmas. No presents—just love and happiness with family and friends—and no mess to deal with… Over the years, I've decided Christmas wasn't worth it. Nowadays, I joke that I'm cursed, but in reality, I'm more immune to its charm. I usually spend a few days with my sister and her family, and that's about it. No big fuss or party. I'm okay with it… Anyway, I prefer working while everybody else celebrates. Christmas is something you share with the ones you love…your wife, your children, your family… Celebrating it while being single isn't quite attractive."

Aisha blinked in the dark night, wrapping her arms around her folded legs. "Whoa, that's a lot of coincidences. I don't believe in them, but right now it's either that, or Santa cast a spell on you for real. Were you a naughty kid? The man is known to have a blacklist. There's no other sensible explanation for your streak of bad luck."

I breathed out a laugh. "I don't believe in coincidences either. We have that in common. And yes, I was a very nice kid growing up. A little on the hyperactive side, but other than that, I never gave my parents any trouble."

She grinned, and the quiet comfort we shared beneath a sky full of stars made me want to kiss her. To hold her. And to fix that smile on her lips. Even though we hadn't known each other long, the way her arched lips moved just now, along with the peaceful expression on her face, revealed a glimpse of her real self—not the guarded celebrity, nor the bitter woman frustrated with Christmas that I'd come to know until now.

A flicker sparked in her eyes. Her irises gleamed, and I held my breath as she edged closer.

Chapter 7
Aisha

"**W**ould you mind holding me?" I asked. "I'm not ready to go, but I'm shivering." Gavin stretched out his legs, opening them just enough so I could squeeze my body between them. He enveloped me with his arms, my back pressing his muscled front. "Better," I said as we watched the reflection of the moon over the ocean, the breaking waves resembling ribbons of diamonds.

"You live far from here?"

"Boston. I'm an art therapist. For kids on the autism spectrum. I went to college there and stayed afterward. Those kids are my life."

I turned in his arms. "Wow, this is amazing. Truly. And for the record, I pictured you as a math teacher. Or maybe a biologist. Not an artist." I studied him for a long moment. "You have that geeky look up close. A child therapist who hates Christmas. Mm-hmm. Interesting."

Gavin let out a warm laugh. "I don't hate Christmas. I'm just not a fanatic. And I don't make a big deal about it. It doesn't mean I can't appreciate it when I have to. If you gimme an out, though, I'll take it. Not tempting fate on purpose."

We watched the ocean for a few minutes, the waves crashing in the dark composing the only melody around us.

Gavin cleared this throat after a moment. "Don't freak out, okay?"

"I won't." I twisted around in his embrace to watch him.

"When I was a teen, I kinda had a thing for you…"

My heartfelt laughter smoothed the frown across his face.

"You did? You had a crush on me?"

"Big time. It's strange, having you here with me like this. My younger self would have been ecstatic." He let out a chuckle. Was he embarrassed about it?

"Wait. You were into pop music?"

Gavin ran a hand over his short stubble and wrinkled his nose, but said nothing.

"Oh." Realization hit me. "You didn't—?"

"Huh… Sorta."

"Whoa, you hated my music?"

He gave me a little shrug and a clenched-teeth smile. "Sorry?"

"Gavin Moore. Please don't tell me you're a rock fan, or even worse, a metalhead?"

The man raised both hands. "Come on, you can't impress girls at sixteen if you listen to an all-girl pop band and you have a thing for the lead singer. I had my street cred to live up to. Rock it was. But then you switched to country, and I don't know, it sounded better. More like you…somehow. To be honest, I might have listened to a few tracks. Please, don't tell anyone because I will deny it, even under torture."

Laughing, I pressed both hands to my warm cheeks.

"Gosh, I can't believe you said that. Ohmygod, I bet you loved the short skirts and cropped tops they made me wear."

Gavin's arms fastened around me. "In fact, remember those pink plaid shorts with the white blouse tied at the front you had on one of your album covers? That was my favorite outfit. Thinking about it spiced up many of my nights." He winked, and I almost dissolved right there.

I coughed a laugh. "Too much information. God, teen boys. You men are all perverts." I shook my head. After a moment, the laughter died down, and the air around us thickened. "What about your older self? Is he disappointed I don't live up to his expectations?"

Gavin cocked my head to the side with a finger and gazed at me with something I couldn't describe but filled me with pure joy. "No. You're a star, Aisha. In more ways than you know. The reality is much better than kid-Gavin's expectations. I'm glad I'm getting a chance to know the real you. The one without the cameras or sparkling outfits. The one without all the glam and superficial stuff."

His words acted like a balm to my bruised heart.

In a swift movement, I reached to the side and fished a small brown bag out of the purse I'd bought earlier. "Thank you for saying that. People don't usually see me for who I am."

"And for what it's worth"—he twirled a curl of my hair around his finger—"I prefer your hair wild and curly."

"You do?" I asked.

"Yes."

A few seconds of silence floated between us.

"Thanks. For seeing the real me." I offered him a soft smile. "This calls for a treat."

Gavin watched me, his brows arching in surprise.

"Churros," I said as I gave him a piece of pastry. "And"—I took out sample-sized alcohol bottles—"drinks."

I twisted the cap of two and handed him one.

We clinked our booze samples.

"To a normal afternoon and night on this crazy island. Thanks for making up for my shitty day. You're a special kind of someone."

I scrunched up my face as I downed the vodka.

"When did you get these?" he asked.

"When you were busy discussing the shuttle with that old man earlier. Oh, what time is it?" I checked my phone. "Ten eighteen. Gavin, we missed the last one. It left like twenty minutes ago."

"Guess we'll walk then," he suggested, rising to his feet and holding out his hand to me, not bothered by the idea of it. "Come on, beautiful star, shine upon me and show me the way. We have over ten miles to go."

"Don't put me on a pedestal. I'm a flawed woman. Let's just call a cab."

Gavin shook his head. "Sorry. I checked. There's none on this island. The guy who drives the shuttle is the same man who sings at another resort bar on the other side of the island on weeknights. People don't venture out of their hotels much around here. No nightlife or anything to entertain tourists at night. Locals must walk or ride bikes… I don't know. Either way, they don't seem like they want or need cabs."

I blinked. "Gosh, I thought you were joking when you said we'd walk back to Las Palmeras."

"No. And to get back to what you said about flawed.

You're special, Aisha. It has nothing to do with fame. You just have that aura surrounding you. It's magnetic."

I tugged at his hand and ignored his words, even if they sent gentle waves of bliss rolling through me. And warmth. And slivers of desire. "Okay, then. Let's go. Do you think we'll make it back to the hotel before the morning?"

"Don't worry, I'll carry you if it comes down to that," he said, not answering my question. In all honesty, I had no idea how far we were from our hotel and was in no hurry to get back there. Right now, Gavin's company was all I cared about. Being with him pushed away the dark Christmas clouds that had been hovering over me for the last three years. With a sigh, I put my flip-flops back on, and with my hand still nestled in his, I followed Gavin in the inky night and handed him another drink for the road.

———

The next evening, I sat at the bar wearing one of the outfits I bought yesterday, a purple A-line summer dress that made me feel good about myself. No more ginger-bread-themed pieces of clothing for me. Tried it. Hated it. Case closed.

Last night, Gavin and I came back to the resort when the sun was about to rise, drunk and laughing like kids. I'd slept in until noon, enjoying a lazy morning for once—not in a hurry to leave the comfy cloud that was my bed.

Early this afternoon, when I went to get my stuff from the locked safe in my flooded hotel room, I learned I would have to spend the rest of my vacation at Las Palmeras. Gavin had been right all along.

Once again, I wanted to call Riley and ask him to fix this, but I didn't. Nah, my ego stepped in just in time. I wasn't ready for him to tell me I should've stayed in town or that Scooter should have tagged along.

Nope. Not ready to be lectured or forced to assess my disdain for the holidays once again. Last year, my manager had suggested another shot at therapy after I had a meltdown about a Christmas fundraiser he wanted me to attend. I refused. Nothing could change the way I felt about that period of the year. I didn't need to be saved. It was all good—as long as I stayed away from Christmas cheer.

Instead, here I was, doing what I could to enjoy my stay in Christmas Land and hoping to spend more time with my new friend, the man I couldn't stop thinking about. The one who had shown me yesterday how selfless he could be, wanting nothing more than to make sure I had a great time and a new wardrobe that would make me happy.

I snickered behind my hand, a flush slowly crawling its way up my face when his words about having a crush on me a decade ago replayed in my head. Gavin looked sweet and vulnerable when he admitted it. When he called me a star, a flutter of butterflies danced in my stomach, free from any fame-related meaning, but charged with something different. On our way back here, I caught him watching me with a blazing intensity that had weakened my knees. Perhaps I'd dreamed it. Had I?

Uneasy with the thought, I blew out a breath, pushing it aside. It was probably the booze that had sent my imagination—and hormones—running wild.

Under the disapproving gaze of the bartender, I snapped back to the present moment and ordered a dirty Martini, ready to drown my sorrows. And my silly thoughts.

He watched me, a disapproving frown on his face.

"What? We're all not into the holiday mood."

He shrugged. "Didn't say anything."

"C'mon, you didn't have to. Your contempt is written all over your face."

The bartender whirled around, leaving me there to sulk on my own. I gave his back a nasty glare, my annoyance about this place reaching new highs.

A man in his late forties, dressed in a condescending attitude and a white shirt covered in multicolored snowmen, neared me. "Is this place taken?" he asked, his chin pointing to my left, pulling me out of my cynicism.

Great. I didn't need the company. I was not in the mood to chitchat with another Christmas guru. The polite side of me won, and I forced a tight bend to my lips. Deep inside me, I wished Gavin would show up. We hadn't talked all day; he was too busy taking part in Christmas challenges with his elderly friends. For a reason I couldn't explain, after the hours we spent together yesterday, I missed hanging out with him. And selfishly, I wished I were the only friend he spent his free time with.

"Is this seat taken?" the man repeated.

Would it be rude to pretend I was saving it for someone even if said someone never showed up? There was just something about this place that made me want to shut the world out. As if I could be mean on purpose... Once again, my nicer side won the inner battle.

"Nope. All yours," I said, guzzling half of my drink in one sip.

"Why aren't you dressed for the occasion?" the man asked.

Why do you care? I wanted to say. *Geez, people, give me a break.* The more time I spent here, the more I realized this hotel was like a cult or something.

I closed my eyes for a second and breathed out, trying

to keep my annoyance under wraps. "I'm good. No worries."

"Oh, you're one of those *I hate the holidays* people, aren't you?"

"Busted."

Now, you can walk away and let me enjoy my martini. Alone, I told him in my head, bringing my attention back to my drink, toying with the napkin used as a coaster.

"Why not?"

Why wasn't he getting the memo? Not here to chat, my friend. Here to have a drink. And to forget tomorrow is Christmas Eve and I'm not going to get the vacation I hoped for.

"Long story."

Clipped answers, man. It means move along. It's flirting 101. Go annoy someone else.

The man leaned forward and brushed my arm with his thick fingers, his breath warm on my cheek. A chill traveled ran down my spine. The bad kind. "I have all night. A pretty woman like you shouldn't sit here all by herself."

"Whoa," I sighed. Even his flirting sounded bad. "Don't make assumptions about what a woman like me wants."

The bartender placed an eggnog decorated with a cinnamon stick before me. A shiver of disgust shook me. I raised a finger before he could walk away. "Sorry, huh…" I searched for a name tag.

"Vlad."

I snapped my fingers. "Right. Vlad. Sorry, but I didn't order this."

"I know," he said, his tone doing nothing to hide his smugness. Again.

"Hello? I don't want it. Take it back."

"Miss, it's a gift. It would be rude to refuse."

"From whom?" The person sending it to me clearly

had no idea it was wrong on all fronts. Probably another lonely man looking for company. My annoyed expression was clearly not enough to scare them off. *Not here to be social, people*, I wanted my face to say. *Stay away.*

"The gentleman across the bar. He told me it was your absolute favorite."

My gag reflex kicked in when I dared another look at the awful cocktail set before me.

My favorite. Yeah, right. Nonsense. The folks here were downright bonkers. Nothing else could explain their obsession with a big fat man dressed in red and his stupid holiday.

My eyes narrowed to slits as I tilted my head to see who could be naive enough to think I would ever drink this horrible thing that had no right to even be considered alcohol.

Gavin, dressed in a dark-green shirt, flashed me a cocky grin. One that could lead me to murder him. In his sleep. With my bare hands.

If only he weren't that good-looking. Or that nice and selfless. Or smelled so divine. And probably my only friend in this hell.

Arghhhh…

Our eyes met. His twinkled in the distance. My exasperation increased when he held up his own drink. A beer. Prick.

I ran my tongue over my lips as curses jumbled around in my head.

"You should take it back to him," I told the bartender. "It's *his* favorite." The man studied me for a second, and without saying anything, probably because he realized it wasn't a good idea and was already tired of my complaints, left with the white drink, moving in Gavin's direction. I raised my martini and chugged the rest, my eyes locked on his.

Gavin snickered as Vlad placed the glass in front of him with a shrug.

"Where were we?" I asked the man next to me, pretending to be interested in him, doing my best to avoid Gavin's piercing gaze as it burned my skin from where he sat.

"That you shouldn't be—" He got interrupted when the barman handed me a glossy red drink with a white foamy topper in a flute.

"Whoa, what's that?" I asked with a grimace, lifting my eyes to him.

"A melted Santa."

"A melted what? Are you doing this on purpose?"

Vlad leaned against the counter behind him, his arms folded over his chest, one eyebrow tipped up. "You're not going to make me take it back again, are you? The man said this was a safe choice."

I choked on a cough. "Melted Santa, this is ridiculous. I don't do Christmas. Take it back."

The barmaid shook his head. "Sorry, not this time. The mister told me you'd say that, but to deny your request. I can't help you. Enjoy."

He winked at me and moved to the side, nearing a couple, leaving me there, jaw hanging open, eyes wide open, and speechless. I didn't know whether to laugh or cry. Laugh it was.

A melted Santa. Okay, one point for Gavin.

I tipped my head back, laughing. Tears welled up in my eyes.

Once I regained my composure, my gaze found Gavin, and he offered me a victorious smirk, raising his beer again.

How did he manage to chase my grumpiness away that easily? I got to give it to him. In his company, I felt like myself again, like the person I was up until a few years ago. Back then, I was always ready for a comeback and enjoyed some harmless fun. Right now, my mind savored the idea of crafting the perfect plan. Yeah, in that instant, Aisha Jones—the real, original me—was back in full force.

After he finished serving people around me, I waved the bartender over. "Send the man the flashiest pink cocktail you can make. And tell him it's called plaid shorts, circa *That Boy*. He'll understand. Also, it's his birthday, so make it super special. Impress me." *That Boy* was the album where I wore the plaid pink shorts on the cover Gavin said he fantasized about as a teen.

Vlad gave me a weird look but mixed boozes, ice cubes, and juices to create my pink request, bright enough to glow in the dark. Absolute perfection.

Before he delivered my personalized order to Gavin, Vlad pressed a button on his phone, and "Feliz Cumpleaños," a Christmas-like version with bells and a chorus, started playing. He made a cupcake appear from underneath the bar and lit up sparklers.

Oh. My. Freaking. God.

This was even more perfect than anything I could have imagined.

I shifted a bit to the right, not wanting to miss a second of my friend's reaction.

People around the bar sang along as Gavin, his face lightly flushed, glanced all over with bunched brows. When our eyes locked, confusion swam in his blue eyes, and the wrinkle across his forehead deepened. Wearing my best smile, I lifted my drink and mouthed, *Cheers*, in his direction.

Once the song ended, Gavin and the bartender

exchanged a few words, and the latter must have repeated what I said because Gavin spat the beer he'd just sipped.

My gaze never wavered from them, as I enjoyed this little revenge of mine a tad too much. Gavin blinked my way, and I shot him a big, victorious smile, wiping off the new batch of tears filling my eyes with a napkin.

Beside me, the man, whose name I still didn't know and forgot all about, inched closer, his breath now tickling my neck. "Honey, ignore that man, he's—" His voice got drowned in the noisy bar, my focus a galaxy away from him.

A genuine smile broke free on my face the moment Gavin approached us minutes later, another red and white drink in hand. And that sexy smirk plastered across his lips.

"Hey, Mags. Thought you could use a friend. And a little fun. Oh, and I brought your favorite drink over."

I pinched my lips to avoid chuckling.

Heat stirred in my lower abdomen.

This cocktail-war between us had been making me feel things I shouldn't.

My entire body combusted at the idea of spending the rest of my night with Gavin, far from here.

How did he become so crucial to my good mood in a matter of days?

Beside me, the annoying man—*for God's sake, couldn't he just leave?*—pivoted to face him. "Sorry man, she's busy. With me." His gaze traveled between Gavin and me. "Wait. Are you—? I thought you were... Oh, I'm mistaken. Your name is Mags..." He scratched his temple, looking confused. "As in Maggie?"

I nodded. With maybe too much enthusiasm. "Yep. At least it was the last time I checked. I can call my mother to ask her if you want." White lies wouldn't hurt.

The man's eyes rounded. "Huh...I thought you were

someone else. Sorry I've been bothering you. I-I'll go now." Without another word, he turned on his heel and left.

"Jerk," Gavin exclaimed, making a martini appear from behind his back.

Finally.

I was probably grinning from ear to ear now. "Thank you. You're the best. Now we're talking." I took a sip, and a moan escaped my lips.

"I love the effect I have on you," Gavin said.

I backhanded his chest. Under his intense gaze, I felt my cheeks catch fire.

"About that loser… Don't worry, okay? There are creeps everywhere."

A loud chuckle left my mouth. "His face when you called me Mags. It was worth every penny in the world. Gosh, I wish I had it on camera."

Gavin's clear baritone laughter mixed with mine. "It was time for him to go. The fun had lasted long enough."

"Someone is being jealous?"

"No. Someone is watching out for you. I saw how he undressed you with his eyes."

I chewed on an olive. "And how did he look at me?"

"Like you were his favorite holiday snack, and he was starving."

"Ohmygod, this is the lamest metaphor I've ever heard," I said through a chuckle.

"Did you forget I work with kids for a living? They have the same look when they are presented with candies. No mistake here. By the way, thanks for the cake. I never imagined a whole bar would sing happy birthday to me in Spanish during the holidays. Because of you, I can check this from my bucket list."

I curtsied. "You're very welcome."

"By the way, I think that drink will become my favorite

one. Vlad even gave me the recipe. I loved the attention." He smiled with those sinful lips of his.

"Oh, he did?"

Gavin nodded.

"This night is so weird. Want to get out of here?" I asked, wiping the new tears forming in my eyes from laughing so much.

"Woman, I thought you'd never ask."

Gavin grabbed my hand, and just when we were about to escape the crowded bar, he got surrounded by a bunch of older people, looking at me with interest. Or analyzing me. It was hard to tell as they gave me slow once-overs. I crossed my fingers, hoping they wouldn't recognize me.

"Gavin," a lady in her seventies said, stepping forward and patting his arm. "You haven't introduced us to your friend. That is so rude." She moved to the side to face me. "I'm Ruth." She turned toward her friends. "This is Tea and Dolly. And this is my husband, Gaston. We've been married fifty-two years." They exchanged a glance that made my knees go weak.

I cupped my heart with one hand. "Wow, fifty-two years. This is impressive. I'm Ais—Maggie," I said. "Nice to meet y'all. How do you know Gavin?"

Beside me, my friend rolled his eyes, and I pressed my lips together to avoid smiling.

Ruth let go of his forearm and took my hand instead. "Mr. Gavin is helping us win all those Christmas challenges. The other day, he built a Christmas tree with us, and this afternoon, we made a gingerbread house. He's so talented with anything Christmas. And so tall and handsome. Those biceps. And that toned body." A loud clearing of throat from Gaston silenced her mid-gush.

I had to grin at that. Gavin had a fangirl.

"Yeah. He is all that and more. And helpful too," I agreed.

"Oh yes." Ruth lowered her voice. "Dorothea and Callista got super jealous when we recruited him. A good thing, I tell you. They won the Christmas tree contest three years in a row. With Mr. Gavin to distract them, we had a great chance to win. He's so young; they couldn't pull their eyeballs away from his body the other day." The women cackled, and Ruth high-fived her friend Tea. I failed to contain my giggle. Where had I landed? What was this place? Older people were acting like third-grade kids. For once, it was refreshing.

"Gavin is a very generous man." My eyes met his for a fraction of a second, and the way his shone warmed up my insides. "I'm glad he's helping you out."

"We were actually heading out for a night stroll," he told them. "Can we talk tomorrow?"

Ruth bobbed her head. "Sure. You kids have fun."

I mirrored their smiles. "And it was nice meeting all y'all."

Gaston moved forward, standing beside his wife. "You two have to come to our Christmas Eve celebration tomorrow night."

Just the words sent a surge of acid up my throat. "That's very nice of you, but I don't do Christmas celebrations."

The collective jaws of the elderly teens hit the floor, and they almost popped their eyeballs out.

"You. Don't. Do. Christmas?" Ruth repeated, articulating each word.

Gavin snickered, and I nudged him in the ribs with my elbow. Hard. He was not helping.

"We'll be there. Count us in. Gimme an hour or two to convince Mags it's a good idea, though."

I spoke through clenched teeth. "No, Gavin. Not going."

He pulled me aside. "Mags, you need to let loose for a night. Enjoy some harmless fun. It's only Christmas Eve. It kinda doesn't even count. If I can do it, you can too. We'll have each other to be miserable with if it's bad. Look at their faces. How can we say no to them? It will be fun. I'll make sure of it. They are real chatterboxes and can't stop gossiping, but they are nice people. They will keep you entertained. It will be like having family here with us for a night. And if you wanna leave, you tell me, and we'll go. I promise."

I closed my eyelids and massaged my temples. So far, my vacation looked nothing like I had envisioned.

Gavin grabbed my shoulders. "I'll have your back, okay? Don't overthink it."

"You're lucky you took me shopping and gave me a piggyback ride when my flipflop broke last night."

He leaned closer and whispered, "And it was my pleasure. You couldn't possibly walk in those heels you bought while drunk. Plus, you fed me the entire time you were perched on my back. I'd never complain."

My body quivered at his words. Heat waves rippled through me. This made no sense, none at all, but I relished how Gavin's proximity made me feel. His presence was like a balm, easing the tension in me but also scorching every inch of my flesh whenever he stood too close.

I blew out my discomfort. Then inhaled again, addicted to his scent, pure ocean and musk, something exclusive to him. Okay, why was I lying to myself? The discomfort was nothing compared to the mix of excitement and longing billowing inside me. Something I hadn't experienced in a long time, as I was desperately trying to keep my heart safe from being shattered again.

Gavin turned to face the group. "We'll be there." He looked at me from the corner of his eye and reached for my hand. *It will be all right,* he mouthed.

Could he sense the throbbing of my pulse racing through my fingers? It felt like my vital organ was digging its way out through my ribs.

"Is there a dress code?" I asked them, the taste of despair now coating my tongue, leaving a track of fire behind.

Ruth clasped her hands. "The more Christmassy, the better. Surprise us, dear." She squeezed my free hand between hers. "We'll have dinner together, then go to that dance party in the garden." She grinned at Gavin before bringing her focus back to me.

I nodded, my jaw so tight, my molars were at the risk of fusing together. "Can't wait," I said, feeling my skin break out in hives at the idea of wearing a Christmas outfit and partying with a bunch of strangers. Ugh.

As if he sensed my uneasiness, Gavin didn't release my hand after wishing Ruth and her friends a good night.

"Are you serious, right now? You trapped me. If it's a prank, come clean. Now."

Gavin's hold on my hand grew tighter. He drew circles over the pulse point on my wrist with the pad of his thumb. "It's not. How could we say no to them? They've been good to me since I got here. It's just for a few hours… Don't worry. Nothing bad will happen. I'm the cursed one, remember?"

I slapped his chest. "Ha. Ha. Funny." My pulse rate went ballistic, my limbs went numb, and air stopped reaching my lungs. There was nothing funny about having a Christmas Eve dinner with a bunch of strangers.

I breathed in, trying to ease the tension crawling up my

back and wrapping around my skull. Now wasn't the time for a migraine. I exhaled, trying to get rid of the discomfort swirling inside me.

"No prank, Mags. If we're stuck here, the best way to entertain ourselves is to enjoy at least some festivities."

"Ohmygod, you're impossible." Gavin let out a warm laugh. I elbowed him. Harder this time. "It's not funny, Gav. I already told you I hate Christmas. I still can't believe I'm stuck on this island, in this hotel for two weeks. It's the worst possible scenario."

"Not being overdramatic, I like it." He winked, and some of my wrath left me.

"Oh, you've seen nothing."

He stopped in his tracks and swiveled to face me. "What did Santa do to you? You must have a good reason to hate Christmas that much?" He tucked a strand of my hair behind my ear, and shivers ran through me. The exciting and fuzzy kinds.

I pressed my cheek against his palm, relishing the warmth for the short second it lasted. "Long story. Not my proudest moment. No need to dwell on the past." I averted my eyes, blinking away the watery fog clouding them, my thoughts doing a tug of war in my head. Emotions coiled inside me. Deep down, I was scared. Afraid the memories of that day would resurface if I indulged in anything Christmas-related.

The way Gavin watched me thawed something inside me that had lain frozen all these years. It was in his eyes. The way he looked at me. I felt safe. And knew then he wouldn't let anything bad happen to me. On an exhale, I murmured, "I'll come… Tomorrow. But just this time. And only because I trust you."

Saying those words out loud removed a thousand

pounds off my back but gave me palpitations and brought more tears to my eyes.

Why was I agreeing to this? Oh yes, because I would do anything to avoid talking about what had happened on that day three years ago. Nope. Not going there. It hurt too much the first time; I wasn't about to relive that episode of my life.

"I hoped you'd change your mind. It's a date then?" Gavin asked, a mischievous smile stretching his lips.

"Whatever. It's just you messing with all my self-imposed rules. And enjoying every minute of it." I sighed and walked away, searching for a breeze, some fresh air to dissipate the knots twisting my stomach, the tension in my back now moving along my arms and crippling my neck.

"Mags, wait," Gavin called after me. "If you don't wanna go, we won't. We can do something else. You don't need to do anything you're not willing to. I'm sorry I put you on the hot seat."

I stepped back to face him and liquified inside at his expression. Some of the knots loosened. Gavin was genuinely sorry.

The war inside my head picked up again. Perhaps he was right, and it was about time I overcame my fears and got out of my comfort zone. My mom and Riley had been telling me for years. Were they right all this time?

My voice sounded weak as I spoke again. "I'll go. I-I think I can do this. Just this one time, though. For what it's worth, you are right. As long as I'm stuck in this place, it's better to have friends to rely on. It could maybe make this whole stay worth it... Almost."

We stared at each other for a second too long, and my pulse kicked up, igniting my blood and playing with my self-control. Warm, fluffy feelings spread inside me. My smile broadened.

Gavin grinned. "I'm glad you changed your mind and aren't ready to kill me, because I have something you might actually like."

Chapter 8
Gavin

With a pep in my step, I hurried to the front desk. The stars must have been aligned because Luciana was still working at this hour. The woman was a friend of Ruth and Gaston—they'd been coming here to celebrate the holidays for almost a decade now, so people around here knew them pretty well. And let's just say Ruth had a way of making an impression on people. After I explained my plan, Luciana rearranged the next morning's schedule to accommodate my request.

"Thanks," I said, offering her a generous tip.

"What's the surprise?" Aisha asked once I joined her in the lobby.

"Tomorrow morning. You and me, we'll go somewhere."

She gave me a quizzical look, her arms folded over her

chest, and rolled her jaw back and forth as she studied me. "What should I wear?"

"It doesn't really matter. You won't stay dressed for long."

Her eyes grew big. "Gavin."

"Relax, it's not what you think. You'll love it. I swear."

Minutes later, we sat on the cold sand on the deserted beach, the tide washing our bare feet, and the warm breeze sweeping our skin.

"How is it?" I asked.

"How is what?"

"The stardom? Being rich and famous? Don't you miss being anonymous sometimes?"

Aisha fiddled with a piece of seashell between her fingers before tossing it in the water. "The truth? I've been doing it for so long, I can't even remember what my life was like before. This is my reality. Sure, some days I wish nobody knew about me, and that strangers would let me be when I do grocery shopping. But"—she shrugged—"I guess it's part of the game. But I love vacations like this, far from the rest of the world, where I can just be myself."

Her words twisted my heart. I leaned in toward her, so we were almost looking right at each other. "In my opinion, it's kinda sad."

"Why?" Her dark irises sparkled like the most precious diamonds in the soft glow of the moonbeams.

"Because. Don't get upset, it's just an opinion. You shouldn't have to come to an isolated place like this to be yourself. You should be allowed to be yourself wherever you are. And you should be able to eat anywhere without ending up on a gossip website or a magazine cover."

"Yeah. Some people have it far worse than I do. Take my friend, Carter Hills, for example. The press used to love to depict him as a broody bad boy with an attitude. He's the most selfless and genuine person I know. And yet, no matter what he did, for years, the stories got blown up a million times bigger than they should have been, and the media tracked him everywhere. I'm lucky fame isn't after me this way. So, I guess it's not that bad at the end of the day."

"You're probably right."

I filtered sand through my fingers as we stayed silent for a long beat.

"How is it? Being an art therapist? Working with kids must be pretty awesome, but there's a bad side to everything."

My breath caught in my chest, and titanium coils wrapped around my stomach. Deep breath in. Deep breath out. Avoiding Aisha's eyes, I ran a hand over my face. My throat worked. I swallowed, summoning the courage to speak the next words.

With a hint of a smile grazing her lips, Aisha watched me as if I could do no wrong. The same way my little patients looked at me.

"In general, it's great. But on my way here"—my throat itched, and I wished I had a beer to soothe it—"I learned we lost part of our funding, and we had to let four children go. Mere days before the holidays... They have been doing so much progress, thanks to music and painting. Now the office is closed for the week, and there's nothing I can do about it. The worst part was that I didn't even get a chance to say goodbye or find a way to make things right." I paused. "Children's access to treatment shouldn't depend on their parents' income or subsidies... It's unfair. I'll never get used to this. In a way, I feel like I'm the one who failed them and their families. Early patient care makes all the difference with these kids. Now they're on their own."

Aisha scooted closer and grabbed my hand in hers, the heat from her palm traveling through me. "You're right; it's unfair. Sorry, Gavin. I didn't mean to open that door. For what it's worth, you didn't fail them. The system did. You can't take the blame."

My eyes searched hers. "Thank you, Aisha. Can I call you Aisha when we're alone? I like your name. It suits you much better than Maggie."

"Yeah, I like hearing you say it too. Want the truth, though? I also love being Maggie here because nobody expects anything from Maggie Jones. Can I be her for just a little longer?"

Without thinking further, I cupped her face with one hand and bowed my head, my stare boring into the depth of hers. She shivered under my touch, and it lit up something in my core. "You don't have to pretend to be anyone else around me, Aisha." Her bottom lip trembled, and I forced myself to look away, the temptation to kiss her, here and now, growing stronger by the second.

She closed her eyes and nodded while I wrapped an arm around her shoulders, pulling her to me. With her head resting on my chest and her heartbeat synching with mine, we watched the midnight tide as it caressed the beach.

Once in my room, hours later, I paced the floor of the bathroom, cursing at myself. A part of me regretted not kissing Aisha when I had the chance, but another part of me hesitated, unsure what to do, or whether I even had the right to long to kiss her.

The attraction between us had been instantaneous, growing stronger the more time we spent together. Minutes ago, when I walked her to her room, we just stood there, staring at each other, neither of us able to break the spell that had come over us. When Aisha rose to her tiptoes to drop a kiss on my cheek, I fought with myself not to lean in and just kiss her the way I wanted to. With passion, lust, and a whole lot of desire.

That woman had no idea how irresistible she was. Not a damn clue.

Everything about her was attractive. The way she pursed her lips before speaking her heart out or how she twisted her hair around her forefinger whenever she thought nobody was looking. Her southern drawl that made her husky voice sexy and unique or how her eyes beamed every time her toes bathed in the ocean.

I didn't come here to crush on a celebrity, and Camilla sent me here to reconnect with my Christmas spirit, as she had said. And Aisha Jones hated the holidays with a poignant conviction I had never seen before.

Nothing made sense anymore. Why was I so confused? *Three a.m.*

I should go to sleep. Yet, my mind was raring to go, not at all tired. My thoughts drifted to Aisha Jones for the millionth time, and I feared closing my eyes would erase the memory of the last few hours we spent together.

If we weren't to see each other ever again, those were the moments I wanted to remember forever.

The ease. The chemistry. The yearning.

After a quick trip to the gym to work the angst out of my system, followed by a hot shower and a release that quieted my hormones, I fell butt-naked on my bed, my face buried in the crook of my arm.

Sleep chased away my thoughts. Only to have Aisha's smile haunt my dreams. Her perfect pouty lips like forbidden fruits I could devour till the end of time.

———

Up early, I chatted with Ruth and Gaston in the lobby and picked up coffee, waiting for the woman who starred in my dreams—some of which were far from innocent—to join me.

My heart drummed in my chest, and excitement tickled every cell in my body at the thought of how I'd play my hand later tonight. I had a plan and just needed time to figure out how to execute it. Deep down, I wondered if she would agree with it.

Aisha, Dolly, and Tea came down the elevator at the same time, the older ladies chatting and laughing while the former stood motionless behind them.

"Ready for tonight?" Ruth asked.

We all nodded. From the corner of my eye, I studied Aisha. She looked all kind of uncomfortable beside me as Ruth talked Christmas business. Without a word, I slipped my palm into hers, and she gave it a gentle squeeze.

Whatever happened to her on Christmas must have been bad because Aisha Jones always looked fierce and composed, but now she looked like she'd seen a ghost. Maybe this whole Christmas Eve dinner with my friends wasn't such a good idea, after all.

"You okay?" I asked, my voice low as I leaned in to whisper in her ear.

She nodded. "Yeah."

"You don't look so good. If you want to run away, just say the word. We'll rent a boat and only come back in two days. No Christmas. No dinner. No silly traditions. Nothing."

What could barely pass as a smile curled her lips. "I'll be fine. But don't leave me alone with them. They're way too cheery about the entire thing. It creeps me out a little."

"Not leaving you. Promise." I watched the time on my

phone. "Now let's get going. I owe you a surprise, remember? Follow me."

We left the group and walked to the beach where we entered the tent shaped like an igloo.

"What's this?" Aisha asked, her grip on my hand tightening.

"Don't worry. It's safe."

A man in his late fifties greeted us. "Mr. Moore. Ms. Jones. Welcome to your two-hour massage session."

"Massage? Two hours?" Aisha asked, the shimmer in her dark eyes full of eagerness.

I nodded. "I won a couple's massage gift certificate the other day. After entering the Christmas tree contest with Ruth and her friends. I thought we could use it…together. That it would help you relax."

Aisha jumped into my arms. "You guessed right. Ohmygod, I can't believe you did that. I've been trying to book one for the past two days, but they told me they had no vacancy in the schedule. Gavin, you're my hero."

I looped my arms around her for a moment, relishing the feel of our bodies pressed together. "Merry non-Christmas Eve then. Come on, let's get settled."

Our host led us to the massage tables set next to each other. "Undress and lie down, the therapists will be here in a few minutes."

In comfortable silence, we removed our clothes, our backs to each other. The temptation to watch Aisha undressing made me feel like a teen in gym class, and yet, catching a glimpse of her over my shoulder would be so wrong, but also thrilling. Instead, I focused on my breathing, fearing my dick would betray me somehow if I spun to face her.

Good. I was good. We were good. I exhaled, relieved.

Aisha and I lay down, and with our heads turned to the

side, we gazed at each other. "Thank you," she whispered. "You saved the day."

"Happy I could help. Now let go. Relax."

She stretched her arm, and our fingers touched for a moment. "I mean it, Gavin. You do all kinds of things to make me feel better, and I'm grateful for everything. Just so you know. Thank you."

There. Right there, I would have pulled her into my arms, her legs locked around my waist, and I would have kissed her senseless. Then, I would have spread her on the table and eaten her up for hours because I'd been thinking about doing it. A lot.

Bonus point, because it would certainly help her relax. My treat. Yep, I could be a greedy bastard when I wanted.

My body tensed, and my imagination ran wild. I closed my eyes, chasing my dirty thoughts away. Not working. My dick ignored my plea and hardened instead.

Beside me, Aisha Jones lay half-naked. Nothing could tame the images popping in my head.

If I made a move, would she let me kiss her? Touch her?

On the table, with only a white drape covering my lower half, my body reacting to her closeness, and my mind envisioning everything I wished I could do to her in this tent, I found the entire experience agonizing.

I dragged a hand over my face. God, this couples' massage idea did nothing to tame my aroused self. My painful erection pulsed underneath me, squeezed between my body and the table. I silently prayed no one would ask me to flip onto my back. I writhed, searching for a comfortable position. A surge of warmth invaded every one of my cells, and now my breathing sounded more like panting.

"Are you okay?" Aisha asked from a few feet away. All I heard was a purr followed by "Fuck me."

My Adam's apple bobbed, and I unclenched my fists, seeking some kind of release—something to help me shake off the tightness in my lower body. Let's hope my therapist was a man. With hands larger than a three-hundred-pound football player and a strong masculine scent, negating the sweet tropical scent of Aisha. Yes, the girl even smelled like a wet dream. If a therapist with delicate hands touched me, no doubt I'd break at the seams and expose my arousal to everyone standing too close.

"Gavin, are you okay?" Aisha repeated. "You're groaning."

This time, my brain processed her words.

She extended her arm, wiggling her fingers until I caught them between mine. Some of the pent-up desire left me, and with her hand in mine—her warmth seeping into me—I exhaled for the first time since we arrived. The two of us lay there in silence. The air between us crackled with electricity, the charged particles clinging to our skin, impossible to escape.

Two hours of this would be torture. I screwed myself over by bringing Aisha here with me. Big fucking time.

After a few minutes, our massage therapists walked in, and Aisha let go of my hand. With my eyes closed, I steadied my breathing, already missing her touch while the therapist—a man, thank God—busied himself, kneading every knotted muscle of my back.

Only then did I finally relax, blocking out the soft, delighted moans of the half-naked woman beside me.

Chapter 9

Aisha

"I think even if there was a tsunami alert and they told us to evacuate, I wouldn't be able to move." I let the words out on a sigh out once we settled ourselves on loungers under a palm tree on a deserted section of the beach, the steady crash of waves on the shore easing me deeper into relaxation. "The lady had magic fingers. She melted every muscle until I was nothing but a puddle of bliss. Do you think it's safe to sleep here tonight? I'm not sure I'll ever be able to detach myself from this chair." I adjusted my shades on the bridge of my nose and closed my eyes as the breeze caressed my face. "Thank you, Gavin. For this."

He shifted in his seat, but I kept my eyes sealed, too lazy to even turn my head.

His breathing accelerated, and he cleared his throat.

"Hey, what's wrong?" I asked, now lifting one heavy

eyelid, the reflection of the sun's rays on the water blinding me.

Gavin rose to his feet and sat on the edge of my chair, right in my line of vision. "I've been thinking. We don't have to do Christmas Eve tonight if you don't feel like it. The last thing I want is for you to feel pressured into doing something you're not comfortable with." He raked a hand through his hair, messing it up in the sexy kinda way I liked.

The sight of him, vulnerable, sent a zing to my heart—and between my thighs. Yeah, Gavin Moore stirred something in me. Being attracted to him like this caught me off guard. And it spelled trouble. A lot of trouble…for me.

It took my brain a few seconds to process his words because I was too busy ogling him to fully listen.

With my back straight, I sat cross-legged and squeezed his forearm.

"We?" I echoed.

He wrinkled his nose. "Well, unless you'd rather be left alone, I'm not letting you spend tonight by yourself. It would be rude of me. And as I said, Christmas isn't my favorite time of the year either. As long as we're together, the night will be more bearable, don't you think?"

My pulse spiked at his words. "You would skip on an evening planned by Ruth to be with me?" My heart pounded in its cage at the idea that he'd choose to spend time with me over his other friends.

Gavin gave a single nod. "Anytime." He fixed his gaze on me for a moment before turning his attention to the seagulls battling over a clamshell just a few feet away.

Relax, Aisha. He only suggested spending the evening with you, so you wouldn't be alone. Not to marry you.

I breathed in, caught between the urge to kiss him and holding back. "I wanna go. My name's Maggie, remember.

And Maggie might tolerate Christmas. Who knows? She won't be certain unless she tries. For the record, she's only doing this because you're the one asking her. She really wants to do something nice for you for a change, and it starts with agreeing to be your date tonight."

"My date?" he teased.

Heat swirled in me at the low sound of his voice. "Yes, date. You know, me walking in there wearing heels, my arm hooked through yours, sitting close together… All those little things."

Before I could think twice, I moved to my knees and wound my arms around Gavin's neck. I pecked his cheek, my lips lingering there, the temptation to move them south sending all kinds of signals to my body.

The air froze in my lungs when his eyes met mine. Darker than usual, they sparkled with something I couldn't define. In slow motion, they darted from my lips to my eyes, burning my skin as they drifted up and down. Up and down.

My throat closed. I tried to speak, but the words died on their way out.

Only when Gavin's hands rested on my hips that I realized my arms were still around his neck. "Mags, we shouldn't… Huh, I don't think… Geez, I want to… We-we should go."

Confusion swam across every feature of his face. His words didn't match the heat in his eyes. And the gentle way he clutched my hipbones.

I nodded, still unable to look at anything but Gavin's magnetic blue irises. As if I were in a trance, I couldn't seem to snap out of it.

His throat worked. Even when he'd said we should get going, his hands stayed anchored to my hips, holding me steady and keeping me at a safe distance from him. But close enough so I could breathe him in, all ocean and man, and study the changing color of his eyes.

Gavin pressed his forehead to mine, and we stayed like that, listening to each other's frenzied heartbeats and harsh breathing.

What was going on? Why were we unable to break apart? Of letting go?

"Mags, I want to kiss you so bad right now," he said, breathless, his grip on me tightening, as if to make sure I wouldn't vanish or run away.

My voice sounded foreign when I said, "I want you to kiss me too. And I want to kiss you."

We breathed the same air. Only now, it felt warmer as it filled the gap between us.

"I can't," Gavin said, his voice so low I barely heard him over the hammering in my chest echoing in my ears and the crashing waves on the shore.

"Why not? I want you to. And I know you want it. I've seen how you've been staring at me."

"Because. It will change everything. I'm not here for a holiday fling. If we do this, I won't be able to act as if nothing happened once it's over… This force pulling us toward each other is strong. And I'm not equipped for a heartquake once this vacation is over."

"You feel it too?"

"From the moment I laid my eyes on you when you walked into the dining hall that morning. It has been burning hotter since. I feel like it's my duty to look out for you. To make sure you're okay—and safe. To chase the frown from your forehead and turn those pouty lips up when you're upset."

"Gavin, kiss me." I removed my shades so we could look at each other without anything in the way. Really look at each other. All the way to the depths of our souls. Now he could see that I meant business. That I craved his touch. My bottom lip quivered with anticipation.

He licked the length of it with his gaze while he darted his tongue out and moistened his own lips.

God, he couldn't be more handsome or sexier if he tried.

Gavin leaned in, and just when I thought our mouths would connect, he pulled back. "Sorry. Not happening. It would be wrong."

"Excuse me. Kissing me would be wrong? How?" I leaned back too, my arms falling to my sides.

"Not wrong…" Gavin squeezed his eyes shut. "It didn't come out the right way. What I mean is if I do, I won't stop, and then in about ten days, we'll go back home, and I'll still be haunted by it. Mags, there's a lot more than kissing you that I wanna do." He tugged at his hair. "Fuck, I'll regret it. Damn it." He tilted his head back, staring upwards as if the sky could provide him with an answer.

"Or we can enjoy ourselves for the time being without thinking about what comes next. No strings attached. Once this vacation is over, I'll go back to being Aisha, and you'll go back to the kids."

He brought his attention back to me, and a torn look slid across his beautiful face. "You're not making it easy on me. Fuck, I want to… I really do. But if we're going there, I want all of it. The whole package. Gimme time to think about it, okay?"

I sucked in my lower lip between my teeth. "Please do."

"Mags—"

"The offer is on the table. You take it, great. For both of us. You pass it, no harm done. I don't proposition men in my everyday life. This must be the side effect of becoming someone else. Or that incredible massage you gifted me. Or your presence in my life."

"Mags—"

"And for the record, I wouldn't object to all those other things you wanna do to me. Just sayin'." I winked, heat rising to my cheeks.

Gavin kissed my forehead, his warm lips branding my skin.

Stella, the hotel employee I met on my first day here walked to us, breaking the moment. "Ms. Jones, lunch has been served. As requested. They told me I would find you here."

I lowered the shades over my eyes and moved to stand. "Oh yes. Lunch. Sorry, I forgot. I lost track of time." I pivoted and held out my hand, waiting for Gavin to take it.

"What is this about?"

I grinned because it was impossible to contain my joy around him. And because I loved the questions dancing in his irises. "Surprise. I'm a resourceful woman. Come on."

"I bet you are. Where are you taking me?"

With our fingers entwined, we followed Stella along the shoreline.

Between two palm trees stood a small square table draped in a teal tablecloth, with a bottle of wine and several island specialty dishes beautifully laid out in the center.

Gavin stopped. "Is it for us?"

My smile stretched wider. "Yes."

"When did you plan this? It's… Wow."

"The morning after we went shopping. To thank you for being awesome. Stella helped me to make it happen."

"So that's the dinner you owed me then."

I shook my head. "Nope. This one is just a little extra.

To express my gratitude. You're not getting out of that dinner. Already told you."

He flashed me a soft smile. "It feels like my birthday."

"I thought it was… No, I'm pretty sure it was you being serenaded at the bar last night."

"My birthday is in May. Mistaken identity."

My eyes shrank to narrow slits. "I would've bet it was you."

"Sorry to deceive you."

I traced the length of his corded forearm with my fingertips, and his gaze swallowed mine. At that moment, I ached for him to douse the flames spreading like a wildfire inside me. "Don't be. That guy was a jerk. He tried to win me over with silly drinks. I much prefer your company."

Gavin's stare burned through me. I felt it everywhere, up to my soul. "Happy to hear it. Shall we?" He pulled out my chair and I sat, my body combusting and my toes curling when his lips skimmed my cheek from behind.

I sucked in a shallow breath, fireworks exploding inside me, lighting up every nerve.

———

"Ready to do this?" Gavin asked, hours later, as he stood on the threshold of my room, wearing the most awful ugly Christmas sweater I'd ever seen in shades of red and green, with a three-dimensional reindeer head attached to the front.

"Ohmygod, this is…this, huh…wow… I can't find the words. I was not expecting this when Ruth mentioned a holiday dress code," I stuttered between chuckles as I cupped my mouth with my hand.

Warmth bloomed across my face at the way Gavin looked at me. With a mix of pleasure and lust. Or genuine mirth. Or all three. I had a hard time telling. All I knew was that it took my breath away and sent a surge of warm tingles along my spine and in my lower belly. He'd started staring at me with those hungry eyes earlier when we had lunch on the beach, and their intensity had multiplied since.

I poked his chest. "Close your jaw, big man. I'm not your dinner. You can't look at me like that if you won't agree to our little arrangement."

As if my words acted like a magic formula, Gavin snapped out of it and smiled.

"You're right… Huh…sorry."

"No worries. It's the dress, huh?" I asked, pointing to the over-the-top elf number I'd found at the hotel shop downstairs. Green and white with matching knee-length socks. I also found a candy-apple red lipstick almost matching my precious one, and it injected me with much-needed doses of courage when I applied it.

"No. Not the dress, it's quite something, though. I must say I'm impressed you agreed to play along. Wow. Aisha… it's not the dress but the woman. She's beautiful. *You're* beautiful. And I have something for you. To make up for tonight. I'll give it to you later."

I bobbed my head and blinked, breaking the magnetism that was building up between us. Snaking my arm through Gavin's, I locked my room behind me. Down the elevator, we entered the most epic Christmas display I had ever seen when we landed in the lobby. The giant tree that stood center stage in the room, was now brightened with thousands of white lights. Blue and silver ribbons were wrapped around it, and it looked as if it came straight from the pages of a fairy tale.

I gawked at it, mildly horrified that I was genuinely impressed by a Christmas tree.

"You like it?" Gavin asked, tracing the curve of my ear with his lips, his breath hot against my skin.

I bobbed my head. "This is magnificent. When did they have time to redecorate it?"

He shrugged. "No idea, but it's really impressive." He perused the space around us. "If this were the real North Pole, even Santa would be jealous."

Gavin's optimism was bleeding on me. A lazy smile pulled at his lips as he studied me, and I forgot all about my awe over the tree. He dropped a kiss to my temple and led me further down the room.

Cheerful Christmas music blasted from the speakers in every corner. Servers passed around champagne flutes. Gavin took two and handed me one. We clinked our glasses. For the occasion, the champagne had been colored green. It looked…well, it looked unusual. Thank God, it tasted the same.

"To spending Christmas Eve together," Gavin said. "I still can't believe my sister sent me here, of all places."

"Thanks for doing this with me. If it weren't for you, I would have been locked up in my room, eating my weight in junk food, drinking champagne directly from the bottle, watching horror movies—which I guess are not on the menu in this hotel."

He shook his head. "Nah. They have something like a twenty-four hours a day, seven days a week, three hundred sixty-five days a year Christmas movies marathon going on here. Let's enjoy ourselves. Let's forget it's Christmas Eve and pretend it's just a party."

I nodded.

He grabbed my hand, and I followed him to the dining hall where his friends were expecting us. A sigh slipped from my lips. I was still dumbstruck that we were actually doing this.

A sudden pang of fear gripped me as we neared the table, dressed in a red tablecloth and set with golden plates, and my breathing turned shallow. I tightened my grip on Gavin's arm.

As if he knew just how to calm me down, he whispered in my ear, "It's okay. Relax. It's just a dinner. Nothing more. I'm right here."

I drew in a shaky breath and thanked him. I could do this. Go through this night as if it didn't bring back all those memories I had been trying to lock away for three years now. Fancy dinner. People dressed to impress. Music. No. Not going there. I was strong. Strong enough to resist the urge to relive the nightmare—if only in my mind.

Despite my best resolve, my heart did tiny flips in my chest.

Could I really have a heart attack at this age? I wasn't even thirty. Still, I had to ask myself the question. My feet refused to budge, my heels anchoring me to the cream-tiled floor. Flight, fight, or freeze. Was this what my therapist meant when she talked about fear responses? For once, I was choosing flight over fight. Gavin held me tight, as if he could already feel me slipping away.

The Christmas song playing through the room echoed and bounced around in my skull.

People's laughter and cheers rang out, sounding ten times louder.

Christmas wasn't a happy time. It shouldn't be celebrated with glee. It just felt all wrong.

Something grew at the back of my throat. I scanned the room around me. The lump grew bigger. I rubbed my hands together, chasing away the numbness in my fingers.

People, stop smiling, I wanted to scream.

Oxygen didn't reach my brain anymore.

My body was shutting down.

Coming here was a mistake. I couldn't do this. Not here. Not now. My eyes darted all around me, searching for an exit. Anything to get me out of this place—of this night—and put Christmas behind me. Where it belonged.

This was too much. My chest felt like it would break.

The lump now blocked my airways. I smoothed my trembling hands over my dress.

As if he had a sixth sense concerning me, Gavin leaned forward and kissed my lips. It lasted about half a second, but he did it anyway. The tornado ravaging everything inside me lessened.

In slow motion, I turned to face him, my jaw hanging open as surprise flooded through me. My lips frizzled where his had landed. "What? Why did you kiss me? I thought—"

"Because you looked like you needed it. And there's a mistletoe hanging over our heads. Don't run away just yet, Mags. Please. It hasn't even started yet. Remember, I have your back. Breathe, it will be all right."

I nodded, my constricted airways making it hard to speak.

Ruth approached us and grabbed my arm. "Here you are, my dear. You look fabulous. I'm so happy you joined us. Come on, follow me. We ordered appetizers. I hope you're hungry."

My stomach, twisted so tight it hurt, made the thought of food unbearable, but I bobbed my head anyway, and faked a smile to reassure her that everything was fine. Even if I wanted to speak, the words were stuck in my throat.

I chugged the champagne Gaston handed me after I sat beside him once we all greeted one another. Their little group was wearing matching red sweaters I was certain one of the ladies had knitted herself. They all looked radiant. And so damn happy.

The opposite of how I felt.

Tears pooled in my eyes. This all felt like too much. Though it happened years ago, Christmas had a cruel way of bringing back the hurt—one therapy couldn't quite heal. It just reopened the wound of the humiliation I faced that day.

"You look beautiful," Dolly told me.

I offered her a tight-lipped smile. Right now, I felt ten shades of stupid and ridiculous. My skin itched and my lungs seized up.

Gavin handed me a martini. "Here," he said.

Had I been so focused on trying not to panic that I missed him ordering it?

I swallowed and whispered a "Thank you" his way.

He scooted his chair closer to mine, the heat of his body helping calm the jitters bouncing inside me.

"I'm so happy we're all here tonight," Ruth began. "It means a lot to all of us to have you two celebrating with us this year." I pushed a crab cake into my mouth, distracting myself from her speech. My heart drilled holes into my chest cavity, making a tunnel, ready to escape.

A new song started, the same one I'd listened to on repeat that night when I cried myself to sleep, dressed in a snowy lace dress I couldn't convince myself to remove.

The back of my eyes prickled with burning tears.

No, I wouldn't let those people witness the epic meltdown about to shatter me to pieces.

Unable to sit still any longer, I rose to my feet and excused myself. "I'll be right back," I said under Gavin's watchful eyes as he stared at me with bunched eyebrows, worry clouding his irises.

With a polite nod, I hurried outside, needing fresh air. Air not tinted with Christmas glee and joy. My lungs started working again the moment my feet landed on the path surrounding the donut-shaped pool. From that point of view, I realized I'd been wrong all along. It wasn't shaped like a donut, but a wreath. How could I have missed it? I shouldn't be surprised, and yet.... Las Palmeras had been created from my worst nightmares. Deep inside me, I'd hoped this vacation was a bad dream I would eventually wake up from. Fingers crossed. Gavin's face popped in my head, and now, I didn't wish for it to be a dream anymore. With my eyes closed, I shook my head. I made no sense at all. Everything inside me, including my thoughts, pulled me in different directions and wore me down.

I removed my shoes—heels I'd found with Gavin in that little boutique the other day—and sat down. Lowering my feet into the warm pool water, I exhaled. There. It all felt better here. On my own. Far from the celebrations and the cheerful madness.

With my fingertips, I massaged the back of my neck.

Some of my angst left me, and I breathed out a sigh of relief.

Lost in my mind, I failed to notice someone coming up behind me. I felt him before I saw him. My body seemed to recognize him before my eyes did. My soul already knew him, as if all my senses were attuned to his presence.

His scent filled my nostrils, and like a drug, it went straight to my head. And my heart.

With his shoes off, he sat beside me, tracing figure eights with his feet in the water. "You mind?" Gavin asked in his husky voice that I'd grown to respond to. The one that brought me peace every time he addressed me.

I shook my head.

"You okay?" he asked.

"Yes. No. I don't know. It was just too much in there. I thought I would collapse... I couldn't breathe."

"Mags, what happened to you on Christmas? Did someone hurt you?"

Tears blurred my vision, and I blinked them away. I cast a glance down, not wanting to meet Gavin's eyes. What if he could read me with ease? I didn't want him to see the hurt I'd been carrying around for too long. The humiliation. The shame. The heartbreak.

"Yes. But not in the way you think. Someone made me hate Christmas. And all these people being so fucking happy about it are killing me. My heart is sad on Christmas day. It's broken. Nothing anyone can do about it." I wiped the new batch of tears forming in my eyes. "It's okay. I've learned to accept it. I'm fine the rest of the year. It's just these few selected days that bring back hurtful memories."

He moved, holding my shoulders and forcing me to look at him. "I'm sorry, Mags. Come here."

He wrapped his strong arms around me and pulled me to his chest. To his heart. Where I felt safe. The nagging voices in my head quieted.

His scent enveloped me.

Somehow, it felt as if he knew how to protect me, shield me from pain, and heal the lingering scars zigzagging across my heart. Nothing bad could happen to me while I sank deeper into Gavin's embrace.

"Thank you," I said after a moment.

"As I told you earlier, we haven't known each other long, but somehow, I know caring for you is what I'm here for. In an odd way, we need each other to overcome the pain we both carry around."

"Gavin, kiss me."

"But—"

"No but. It's just a kiss. Not a marriage proposal. Don't—"

Before I could finish, he cupped my face with both hands, his heavy gaze piercing into mine. A whispered "Fuck that" tumbled out his lips a split second before his mouth claimed mine. With restraint at first. And then as if his life depended on it. As if he'd die without a taste of me.

A closed door inside me opened. It freed my heart. It chased my pain away and replaced it with butterflies. And fireworks. And raw bliss.

Gavin groaned into my mouth when he sucked on my lower lip, and my head spun. With one hand around my nape, he deepened the kiss, his tongue pushing to be granted access. A whimper parted my lips, and I let him in. I had never been kissed like this before—like he couldn't get enough of me, and I would need to do this again and again to feel completely satisfied. As if the world might end tonight, and this was our last chance to offer each other comfort.

I twisted his hair around my fingers, and a low growl escaped him when I tugged at the roots.

My breasts swelled. Gavin gained control over my body, our tongues dancing together.

I craved his touch all over me, each inch of my skin screaming to be consumed.

My mind left me. I didn't care about the Christmas Eve dinner or that hotel anymore. Even if bombs had been blowing up over our heads, I wouldn't have noticed.

Gavin brought his hands to rest on both sides of my neck, and I pushed my chest forward. Instead of cupping my breasts, his hands met my waist, leaving a trail of fire and goose bumps on their way down, anchoring me to the moment.

He nipped at my bottom lip, drawing a yelp from me. Our tongues clashed, each battling for control. We were lost in the dance—unable to break apart, unable to breathe away from each other.

Someone cleared their throat behind us.

Immersed in our make-out session, we ignored it.

In my head, I could picture Gavin taking me right here, by the pool, in the dark night, laying me on my back and removing my panties with greedy fingers, a spark flashing in his eyes.

My fantasy collapsed in a blink when the person cleared their throat again, but Gavin kissed along the length of my jaw, down my neck, and across my collarbone, making me forget all about it. I tipped my head back, lids hooded, savoring the ecstasy swirling inside me, and bit my lip as he licked his way back to my mouth.

The person cleared their throat once more, insistent this time. What the hell? Who could be foolish enough to interrupt the best thing that had happened to me on this vacation so far?

For once I was enjoying myself.

Breathless, Gavin and I broke apart. If my face mirrored his, I probably wore swollen lips and heat-stained cheeks.

The man who was tongue-deep inside my mouth seconds ago looked like a teenager who got mauled by a group of hungry cheerleaders. Did I do that to him? A cocky smirk appeared at the corner of his lips, and I had my answer. Yeah, I was to blame. Ohmygod, he looked delicious. Delicious? No other word came to my mind. Fuckable? Yeah, that sounded better.

If only Gavin could see how much effect he had on me too.

"There you are. Thought I'd find you two here," the voice said. The one we still hadn't acknowledged by now. "Are you guys coming back or not?"

Ruth. She stood a few feet from us, her balled fists resting on her hips, looking unimpressed by our starving antics.

Gavin ran a hand over his face, and I leaned forward to comb strands of his hair back into place. No such luck. They preferred their wilder state. I did too. This mussed look suited him perfectly.

"Mr. Gavin? Are you done with the lady? No need to give her a throat exam, she looks just fine to me," she quipped with a teasing tone. "Dinner is served, and we were wondering if you two were coming back."

Ohmygod, did Ruth just say that?

Gavin's gaze drifted to me, and we both burst into a fit of laughter.

With one hand around my shoulder and pulling me to his chest to kiss the crown of my head, Gavin brought his attention to a semi-amused, semi-impatient Ruth. "I'm sorry. The lady here needed some comfort. And you're right. She looks just fine to me." He searched my eyes and winked, and I liquified a little more inside.

We got caught red-handed, making out like horny teenagers, and were scowled at like kids by someone old enough to be our grandma.

Gavin's grin died, and he pushed my hair away from my face, still buried in his chest. "Mags, do you wanna go back or forfeit the entire night? It's your call."

I tilted my head back and lost myself in his blue irises, gleaming in the semi-darkness. "If it's okay with you, I'd like to go back."

He nodded, jumped to his feet, and extended his hand to me. I smoothed my dress with my fingers, puffed my hair, and followed him. Gavin's hand stayed firmly pressed to my back, heat shooting through me in powerful jolts.

The fabric between our skin did nothing to temper the way our bodies reacted to each other.

We joined his friends inside, and the conversation flowed easily between the six of us. I learned their group had started spending the holidays here, all four of them, after Dolly and Tea's husbands died months apart nine years ago. And they've been coming back every year ever since. None of them had children, and had all grown up together. They had been friends for over sixty years.

The entire time we ate, Gavin's hand rested on my thigh. Grounding me. Calming me. I lost count of how many times he asked if I was all right, his breathing caressing the shell of my ear each time, making me hot for him all over again.

"We moved things around while you guys were busy making out," Ruth stated with a wink. "We're attending the dance right after dinner, and we'll do our annual Secret Santa gifts exchange in our rooms later. We don't want you two lovebirds to disappear on us again."

"We're not… It's not…" I stammered, warmth pooling in my cheeks.

Ruth silenced me with a raised hand. "Believe anything you want, but we have eyes, young lady. And we've been on this Earth a long time. We recognize the look of lust…and love."

Once dinner was over, we all rose to our feet. Just as we were about to leave the dining hall, Ruth stopped us.

"Everyone, go freshen up before we hit the dance floor. We'll meet back in the lobby in twenty, next to that giant tree." She pointed to the dazzling Christmas centerpiece standing proud behind her with her thumb.

We all agreed, and Gavin intertwined his fingers through mine before leading me to the elevator. Inside, he wasted no time crashing his mouth on mine, like a starving man who was having a five-course meal for the first time.

My back pressed against the wall, the coolness of the surface contrasting with the heat emanating from that man's firm body as it molded to mine. We were hot molten steel coming together. All my synapses fired. My temperature rose to the point of combustion. I hadn't dreamed it the first time. Gavin Moore could kiss. I fisted his sweater collar, kissing him back with every ounce of desire coursing through my veins.

The elevator stopped on the sixth floor, and Gavin leaned back, his chest rising and falling in quick motions. His dark eyes bore into mine, stealing every drop of oxygen from my lungs. "Wait for me up there. I'll come to get you."

I nodded, heat radiating from me, as the doors closed on him.

The ride to the eighth floor felt like it lasted an eternity…or something close to it. Alone with my thoughts, my brain finally caught up with everything that had happened so far tonight What was I doing?

This, acting on impulse and giving my hormones complete control, wasn't like me. I'd never done anything this carefree before in my life, even when I was younger. Early on, I'd learned there could be a camera aimed at me everywhere I went, so I had always been careful about how I acted. But here, right now, in Las Palmeras, with Gavin, I was living—like, really living—for the first time ever. And I could lose myself in that feeling of freedom. Being Maggie Jones was pretty amazing right now. The happiness tearing through my face was impossible to hide as I entered my room. In the bathroom, I splashed water over my reddened skin, but the smile remained anchored there. It didn't falter. Even after I gave myself a pep talk.

I had no idea why Gavin affected me so much, but I refused to come up with a rational explanation because I thrived beside him. We had a little over a week left to spend with each other, and if he decided that being with me was what he wanted too, I wouldn't lose a minute asking myself pointless questions or wondering how it made no sense. If I needed a reason to doubt myself, I only had to call my mother…or Riley. They usually had that effect on me. Looking at things through a lens I hadn't considered and calling me out on stuff I chose to ignore. But not this time. This time, I was on my own, relishing the freedom my fake identity provided me.

Someone knocked on the door, and I yanked it open to find Gavin standing on the other side with a box tucked under his arm. His boyish smile was still there, making him look even more tempting than before.

No one had ever looked at me this way before, and it was strangely exhilarating. He was sexy as hell, with his sun-kissed skin, gleaming eyes, and that effortlessly messy hair.

Scorching, addictive flames flickered within me at his sight. Powerful enough to set fire to the entire island. Every throb of my heart jolted through me. Nothing else in my life mattered when Gavin stared at me as if his entire world revolved around me.

"You wanna come in?" I asked, my tone lower than usual.

"If I do, we're not getting out. I'm not joking. I'm warning you… If we start this, I'll be all over you," he replied, with a mischievous lopsided smile and brand-new sparks in his eyes, waiting for me to decide.

I sucked in a short breath, my insides churning with exhilaration.

He held my gaze. There was fire in his eyes, and I was the match. "Your call, Aisha."

Chapter 10
Gavin

A tightness grew in my chest as I approached Aisha's room with the box in my hands, wondering if she'd like it. We hadn't known each other long, and yet, when I spotted it in that little boutique the other day, I knew it had been created for her.

I dragged a hand over my face and combed my wild mass of hair with my fingers.

One breath in.

One breath out.

Since I was a teen, I'd always found Aisha Jones kinda hot—and also mysterious—but I'd always assumed she would be pretentious or inaccessible. Child celebrity and all. It was in her eyes. Or the way she smiled. As if she was always on guard, afraid someone might see through her… or worse, judge her. I winced because I missed the right word to describe it.

But in real life, away from the limelight and far from

the rest of the world, Aisha Jones was nothing like I'd expected.

And her true self had been growing on me. Fast. Neither my head nor my heart was prepared for what that meant. The ride would be over before I knew it, and I already feared the aftermath. Perhaps we could be more than a holiday fuck. I couldn't shake away the idea. Aisha had rooted herself so deeply in me, I couldn't see a future where I didn't crave her, or accept the idea of her not being mine.

With one hand still covering my face, I blew on my palm, making sure I smelled fresh.

Another breath in. A roll of my shoulders. And I knocked on her door.

The sight of her stole all remnant oxygen from my lungs when she opened it.

My body tensed at the right places, unable to stay indifferent to the way she looked. And smelled. And smiled. To everything that was her.

"You wanna come in?" Aisha asked in a croaky voice that didn't sound like hers but sent unmistakable signals straight to my dick. It hardened, sucking all the blood from my brain.

I swallowed, forcing my eyes to stay level with her face. "If I do, we're not getting out. I'm not joking. I'm warning you… If we start this, I'll be all over you." My grin broke free as my eyes lingered lower and made their way back up. "Your call, Aisha."

Her clear laughter resonated in the hallway. "I don't wanna be lectured by Ruth twice tonight."

"Let's get it over with, then. We'll come right back here afterward, okay?"

Aisha nodded and stepped closer. I cradled her cheek with one hand like we'd practiced this movement thousands of times before. An emotional earthquake rattled the false sense of calm within me. How would I ever be able to control myself around this woman? She had an effect on me I'd never experienced before. Her full lips parted when she raised her gaze toward mine, pupils dilated and shimmering with unspoken desire.

I lowered my head. "Can I?"

Aisha nodded. "Please, Gavin. Kiss me."

She wouldn't have to tell me twice.

The box under my arm tumbled to the floor, and with one hand still cupping her face, I brought the other around her waist and hauled her to me. Until our hearts connected through our chest walls and our souls found comfort in each other's presence. Until our bodies fused together. Until we tangoed in bliss.

This time, I didn't go slow. Or gentle. I feasted on Aisha's mouth, every piece of me greedy to taste her. Nothing would stop me this time around. Not Ruth or anyone else. Only us, pleasure, and untamed desire mattered.

"Oh, Gavin. Keep doing that… Not that. *Yesss*. This… Oh God," she moaned as I pressed her back to the wall, one hand holding her face still and the other traveling all over her soft ass, straight back, and fisting her hair.

Aisha rocked back and forth over my erection nestled between her legs, spawning a deeper level of hunger for her in my core. Even if we were both fully dressed, I could feel her warmth through our clothes. It radiated through me, playing with every restraint I still possessed.

"Maggie…huh, Aisha…you have no idea what you are doing to me." I traced the length of her jawline with my tongue before sucking on her earlobe. Her movements increased in pace as more whimpers escaped her luscious mouth. "Fuck, I don't wanna go to that stupid dance anymore. I want you. Here and now. In every possible position."

Aisha tugged at my hair roughly and worked her lips back to mine, devouring my face as if she had been starving all these years. Each touch of hers magnified my desire for her, and all my resolves snapped one after the other.

"Keep calling me Maggie. It sounds dirty."

With both hands clasped around her rib cage, I lifted her against the wall until her dress bunched up around her thighs and her legs circled my midriff.

She clutched my sweater with one hand, curling the other around my nape, while I rubbed my hard self against her overheated center, her whimpers doing nothing to tame the beast in me.

I caged her body with mine, my lips still hungry for her —every inch of her.

The fog muddling my brain cleared, and as if stung by a bee, I pulled back.

Aisha's eyes brightened the space around us, casting us in a glow I wasn't ready to move out of. Between ragged breaths, she asked, "What's wrong?"

I brushed the curls away from her face with a finger, waging a silent war with my lips, aching to taste her trembling ones. "Nothing. That's the problem. It feels way too good, and I'm about to humiliate myself here." Aisha cupped her mouth, silencing a snicker. "Yeah, that's how much I want you." Her eyes dropped to my crotch.

"We should go… But—" She raised a finger between us. "You need to wash up first. It looks like you've been attacked by an army of lipsticks. The imprint of my lips are all over that sexy face of yours."

I tipped my eyebrows. "You think I'm sexy?"

A flush covered her cheeks. "Sexy isn't a strong enough

word to describe the way you look and how you make me feel."

"Wanna tell me more about that? What's the right word, Mags?"

Aisha pressed a hand to my chest. "Gavin, I have no idea because I've never felt this before. You'll have to gimme more so I can decide."

"Challenge accepted." We stood immobile, our gazes fused as we breathed in each other's essence, waiting for our horny selves to calm down. "Ready?"

She nodded, and my lips lingered on her forehead for a moment.

In her bathroom, she sat on the countertop, a makeup remover pad in hand. The evidence of our make-out session had vanished from my skin, but the marks left on my heart—and deeper—still pulsed, keeping me on edge. God, how did I end up here with the girl I used to fantasize about during my teen years? In a hotel room. On an island. Ready to fuck each other's brains out minutes ago. I blinked. It didn't make sense…and yet, it made all the sense in the world.

I locked my hands around her waist, relishing the smile hanging from her reddened lips as she cared for me. "What are we doing, Mags?"

She shrugged. "No idea. But I can't wait to come back here later."

My mouth found hers, and our lips molded together.

There was no rush this time. When Aisha's tongue swirled around mine, I indulged for a long minute before pushing back. "Ruth is gonna kill us if we're late," I whispered against her lips.

Aisha offered me a pout, jumped off the countertop, and grabbed my hand. "Come on, Santa. Let's go."

"Can I give you your gift first?"

"You got me something?"

I nodded, capturing her mouth in a quick kiss. "Follow me." Fingers entwined, I guided her toward the bedroom.

Seconds later, Aisha nibbled on her lip as she untied the red ribbon around the box.

A sudden jolt ran through me, and I whispered a silent prayer, hoping I'd made the right choice.

She parted the red silk paper, and her gaze landed on the glittery fabric I couldn't wait to see on her. I held my breath. Her eyes rounded, and a delighted gasp slipped from her lips as her mouth fell open. "Gavin…" A crimson shade colored her cheeks, matching the color of dress hanging from her fingers. Her eyes brimmed and shiny tears. "How?"

She buried herself in my embrace.

"That day we went shopping… You mentioned you had brought along a sparkly red dress along for your trip and that it was probably ruined. I-I saw this when you went to change in the boutique we visited together, and I thought it would look amazing on you."

"But—"

She leaned back, her eyes searching mine. God, she was beautiful, her beauty amplified by the genuine gratefulness glowing in her gaze.

"Merry Christmas, Maggie."

"I-I don't like Christmas."

I shrugged. "Me neither. But can we pretend we do for a day or two? After all, you're Maggie Jones."

I circled her waist with both hands, caressing the curves of her hipbones with my thumbs.

"I guess I could make an exception...for you." She moved to her tiptoes, and brushed her lips against mine. "After all, you gifted me a dress every woman would kill for. I want to wear it now."

"God, I can't wait to see it on you. Why don't you keep it for New Year's Eve?"

"You sure?"

"Yeah, it'll make the celebrations ten times better if I get to watch you wearing it all night."

She sighed, pinching the green fabric over her stomach. "That means I have no way out of this *elfy* thing tonight."

"Oh, you will. I promise."

"You do?"

"It will be my pleasure to rip it off you later."

"God, I can't wait. Let's go before I lock you in here until you follow up on your words."

Hands linked, we made it to the garden. Fairy lights were wrapped around palm tree trunks, and lanterns surrounded the makeshift dance floor. If you forgot all about the reindeers and gingerbread houses scattered across the yard, it looked beautiful. Romantic. Magical.

I wound my arms around Aisha, and we moved together on the dance floor, her arms tight around my neck and her body flush against mine. No doubt she could experience every thick inch of me pressing against her lower stomach. Music didn't even reach my ears, my pulse thrumming too fast. Too loud.

Taking my sweet time, I ran my hand up and down her side, caressing every curve of her body. We swayed together. Aisha purred when my palms connected with her ass cheek, holding her closer to me, leaving no gap between us.

I kissed that spot right under her ear, and she shuddered in my embrace. "You like that?"

She nodded, gasping when I traced the length of her arm. Goose bumps bloomed under the pads of my fingers.

Aisha rubbed herself against my hard self, pretending

to shake her ass, but I knew better. She glanced my way, a challenge in her eyes, knowing exactly how to torture me to oblivion and back.

With both hands on her bottom, I got her to stop grinding, knowing I was close to coming in my pants if she didn't stop her little tease. She grinned, mischief causing her smile to sparkle.

In our own bubble, we forgot about everyone else, our lips too busy sampling each other.

"If Christmas Eve was always like this, I might start enjoying it," I whispered.

"Right now, with you, I don't care what day it is. Just kiss me," Aisha whispered back.

Ruth walked toward us just as our lips hovered a hair's breadth apart. She shooed us away with a flick of her hand. "Kids, just get out of here already. Go have fun. We'll see you tomorrow."

She wouldn't have to tell us twice. I scooped Aisha over my shoulder and made a beeline toward the elevator, her laughter the only sound making its way to my ears along with the pounding of my heart.

I allowed the woman, who I knew had the power to shatter my peace, to shimmy down my body after we entered her room. Standing in front of me, looking like the star that she was, beautiful and dazzling, Aisha undressed, her elf outfit soon on the floor, leaving her in only a set of matching lacy black underwear, her tits pushed up and begging me to give them some much-required attention.

I licked my lips, taking in every inch of her as I prowled in her direction, eating up the distance between us in one stride.

"Ready to play?" she asked, twisting her forefinger between her pearly white teeth.

"Fuck yes," I yearned, discarding my Christmas sweater in a swift movement.

Aisha stepped closer, and with experienced fingers, she slipped the belt out of my trouser loops with a playful *'oopsy'* and a naughty gleam dancing in her dark eyes. My cock grew thicker while she took her sweet time unzipping my pants. She tilted her face up to me, batting her lashes, feigning innocence.

She pushed a hand into my boxer briefs, and my entire world exploded and crumbled at the same time. With my eyes shut, I savored the first contact of her hand around my pulsing flesh. Electricity shot through me.

When I pried my eyes open, the playfulness had left me.

With controlled urgency, I pushed her bra cups down and plunged forward, unleashing the starving animal caged inside me.

And forgetting all about our vacation-fling deal.

Chapter 11

Aisha

Gavin killed me first, then revived me when his lips toyed with my stiff nipples, his strong hands pushing my breasts together, his tongue lapping at me and drawing circles over my flesh. "Mags, you taste like everything I could get addicted to."

I threaded my fingers through his tousled locks, needing something to hold on to as his mouth trailed down to my lower belly. Kneeled before me, Gavin hooked his fingers into my panties and pulled them down in the gentlest way, my body shivering under his dedicated attention.

He brought one of my legs over his shoulder and continued his descent.

Each of my cells electrified.

My breaths came out in pants.

My brain turned to jelly.

My limbs weakened.

With my head tilted back against the wall, I let out a loud whimper when Gavin kissed the patch of the skin behind my knee.

I splayed my hands on each side as one of his fingers traced the wet and aroused seam between my legs and spread my desire all over my folds.

Shivers lined every one of my vertebras.

I bit my lower lip, trying to silence the moans bubbling out when Gavin entered a finger inside me.

He kissed the sensitive skin of my inner thigh, and wild desire blasted within my being when his tongue followed the path to my center.

Nobody had ever made me feel this way with so little foreplay.

Gavin's tongue grazed over my bundle of nerves, and I came in a colorful rush of explosions, unable to lock all the sensations rushing inside me any longer.

"No more playing around," I begged, still surfing the orgasm that shook me to my core.

It usually took me much more to be able to come. But Gavin's magical way might just have healed me of years of climax dysfunction. Oh God. Why didn't I know *this* existed before?

I blew out a winding breath, and my heartbeat hastened in my chest.

Gavin stared at me, still on his knees between my legs. "You okay?"

"Just fuck me. Now. I want that dick of yours inside of me. I wanna see stars. We'll play with each other later."

"Boss much," Gavin teased as he rose to his feet, kicking his trousers and boxer briefs off, before returning his hands to my hipbones. His mouth sought mine, and I could taste me on him. He laid me gently on the bed, not breaking contact with my lips.

Suited in a condom that had manifested without warning—and I didn't care where it came from as long as he wore it—Gavin traced the length of me with his erection, coating itself in my wetness.

Our stares fused. I nodded, and with restraint, balancing his weight on his arms, he pushed himself inside me, inch by inch. The feeling of our bodies connecting for the first time would forever be etched into my memory.

Like we were destined to fit together this way.

The certainty shook me that no one could ever fill me the way he did, and that he might have destroyed me for everyone else.

Chills, shivers, tingles, every sensation known to humankind invaded me.

Gravity ceased to exist, and I was pulled in all directions, my movements fluid and my mind euphoric. I felt my body levitate the moment Gavin slid in and out of me, his self-control vanishing with each thrust.

I saw shooting stars under my eyelids, lightning me up from inside out.

Gavin gripped my hips and growled as he speared into me with everything he possessed.

It was the sexiest thing I had ever witnessed, and the most addictive sound I'd ever heard.

Each time he pounded into me, my yearning for him multiplied. I would never be satiated if we did this only once. His lips crashed on mine, hungry and demanding. In one swift move, he stood up, and I wrapped my arms around his neck, my bent knees hooked in the crook of his elbows on each side.

Strong and steady, Gavin guided my body up and down his thick shaft. The strength of his movements pulsed through me, sending vibrations down my spine.

My clit rubbed against his pelvic bone, and I almost

fainted in his embrace as I lost myself in the pleasure he brought me.

Not giving me any time to recover, he put me back on the bed and shifted me to my side. I lifted one leg over his shoulder, and he rammed into me, one hand curled around my thigh.

"Aisha, I'm so close," he whispered, rolling me to my back and leaning forward to kiss me, his tongue sweeping mine in fast strokes.

"Come in me, baby," I pleaded, my body igniting once more. "I'll… Now," I cried out.

Gavin held my eyes, his body convulsing over mine, a guttural sound leaving his mouth, his teeth tugging at my lower lip.

In slow motion, he lowered his sweaty torso to rest on my breasts, and peppered kisses at the corners of my mouth, on my eyelids, and in that sweet spot under my earlobe. "Is it okay I want to do that again?" he asked, wiping pearls of sweat from his brows with his bare shoulder.

"I would be super pissed if you had said you wanted to stop whatever this is."

He kissed the tip of my nose. "Let's take a quick nap because we'll need our strength to last all night. And right now, there's nothing I want more than holding you in my arms. Gimme a minute, I'll be right back." A moment later, he lay back next to me and pulled me closer, the pad of his thumb circling my still erect nipples, sending new waves of heat down to my belly. His breathing slowed, and I pressed my head in the crook of his neck, his heartbeat rocking me to sleep.

———

"I have an idea," I murmured to a sleeping Gavin, two hours later. I pressed my naked breasts against his side, and his lids fluttered open, a huge smile drawn on his lips when our gazes met.

"Oh yeah?" he asked, his voice heavy with sleep but husky enough to make me feel weak for him all over again.

"Yes. And I think you'll like it. It will be my one-and-only Christmas celebration for this century. You can't miss it. It would be a tragedy. Are you in?"

"What do you have in mind?" he asked, wrapping his arms around me, and hauling me over him, his lips bruising mine in the sexiest way. A surge of desire splashed through me, and I almost forgot what I wanted to tell him.

"I—"

Gavin took control of my mouth, his tongue raw against mine as we shared a consuming kiss. One that replaced all my thoughts with pure bliss.

He kneaded my breasts, and my brain muddled for a few dizzying seconds. He lowered himself on the bed until his mouth could play with my nipples.

"Oh yes," I let out, holding it together by a flimsy thread. The memory of my carefully thought-out plan hit me like a slap, and I forced myself to get a grip. "Stop."

Gavin lifted his face from my chest, eyes searching mine with question marks dancing in his irises, his lips flushed red.

"My celebrations. Huh, I almost forgot… We must focus here."

"Mags, you didn't even tell me what it was?"

I blinked. "I didn't?"

Gavin shook his head, kissing my flesh, a smile stretching his lips.

"Oh. I probably should."

He shifted upward until his eyes met mine, hovering there, waiting.

Oh, yes, that idea of mine.

"It's almost three a.m. I'm sure most people are already in bed. We could 'borrow' a bottle of alcohol from the bar," I suggested, using my fingers to air quote the word, "and go to that wellness igloo where we got those massages… But the two of us this time. Candles. Music. And a middle-of-the-night swim to get started. What do you think?"

Gavin's eyes flashed with a mix of lust and interest. "You like that igloo?"

"Yeah. I wanted to do dirty things to you in there yesterday." His eyes widened. "It was horrible lying next to you like that and not touch you."

"Glad to know we were both in pain."

"I have needs, you know. And you're kind of an eye candy, so… Anyway, what do you say?"

"Being naughty on Christmas day. No wonder you stay away from Santa. Mags, I love how you think." He captured my lips. His mouths possessed mine, and we lost ourselves in the pleasure we brought each other once again. Time stilled. Until he leaned away, releasing a deep sigh that filled the quiet between us. "Okay, I got my fix. For now. Let's go."

Within seconds, he was back in his pants, waiting for me to get dressed. I locked myself in the bathroom for a few minutes, putting the first step of my plan into motion.

I slid my palm into his, and together we traipsed to the elevator, reaching the lobby in minutes.

I was right. Except for an employee at the front desk, the hotel was mostly deserted at this early hour.

"Get us a bottle, and I'll round up some snacks," I said.

"Snacks? Where? How?"

"I can be quite persuasive if I put my mind to it. There must be someone working in the kitchen, prepping breakfast or something. Meet me on the beach in five."

Some inoffensive flirting and the guy in the kitchen let me go with a bunch of treats.

In the moonlight, I followed the beach path, waiting for Gavin in a dark corner, aside from the glow of a lamppost. While he sauntered my way, his eyes gleaming bright and a cocky smirk pasted on his lips, I took the time to study him. Tall, broad shoulders, dark hair. He was everything I would want in my man—and craved. And everything I should stay away from. To guard my feelings. A steady relationship wasn't in the stars for me. Not yet, at least. That kind of commitment wasn't what I was aiming for right now. I aspired to the idea of love, but the last time I gave it a shot, it blew up in my face. Big time. Not that I wouldn't do love again. Some day. Not today, though. Nor the near future.

A warm zing traveled through me at the sight of the man rocking my world and the thought he was mine… for now.

Our gazes met, and it sucked away all the air from my lungs.

Time suspended for me.

At that moment, nothing existed but Gavin.

This was what I should feel all the time when a man— the one I would share my life with one day, when I was ready—looked at me. As if I drew the stars in the sky and was the center of his universe.

My pulse raced in my chest.

My palms got moist.

The way Gavin stared at me made me feel like I'd found my man. *The one.*

But this was all a mirage. A vacation fling. A holiday

fuck. Two strangers needing each other's comfort—and naughty sex—to go through these two weeks on a remote island in the middle of the Caribbean Sea. Nothing more.

"Mission fulfilled," Gavin gloated as his lips touched mine, light as butterfly wings. "Easy peasy. The bartender offered it to me before I even asked." His eyes followed the paper bag in my hand. "What have you got?"

"Stuff. Let's just say it won't be a healthy night," I remarked with a wink. "Even got you another surprise. Just wait and see."

Gavin grabbed my hand, kissed my knuckles, and led the way. "Let's get naughty."

Chapter 12

Aisha

Gavin choked on his breath when I neared him wearing the golden bikini we bought together the other day—paired with high heels and a Santa hat. With my red lipstick on, I knew the effect I had on him.

"Fuck, Mags. You look…you look… Wow," he exclaimed, a twinkle in his irises. "When you said you'd blow my mind with a Santa hat the other day, I prayed for it to happen… Guess Santa has finally granted me a wish."

"That's my Christmas present to you. Told you I had a surprise," I said with a wink.

"You might just have cured me of my Christmas curse. How I wish Santa looks this hot. I'll bring you shopping every day if that's your way of thanking me."

"Three a.m. swim with or without this?" I asked, playing with the string of my bikini bottom.

A mischievous smile appeared on Gavin's face, handsome under the moonlight, an ocean of stars shining upon us.

I closed my eyes for a fraction of a second to imprint this moment in my mind. Gavin. The starry diamond sky. The ocean breeze. The beating of my heart.

A lump grew in my throat. All this was mine. Just for another week.

I blinked to keep the tears threatening to fill my eyes at bay, not wanting to ruin our first night together with downing thoughts. I fixed a smile on my lips just as Gavin brushed the length of my ribcage with his fingertips before resting his hands around my waist.

Electricity traveled through me in powerful currents.

"With. I'll remove it myself. On my own terms. But for now, I love the vision of you in it."

"I thought it might turn you on. Glad I could help you find your Christmas spirit back."

"Woman, you're hot. Do I have to be a good boy, or am I allowed to be naughty too?"

"The naughtier you can be, the greater the fun." I wiggled my brows. "What will it be?"

"I'm about to become the most devilish man you've ever met, Mags."

"Just so you know, this whole role-play thing turns me on. Yeah, I like how it makes me want to be bad too. Come here, Santa."

I surveyed the dark ocean. "You think there are sharks in there?"

"No. I hate those. On my first day, I checked with the staff, and the guy at the reception told me they'd installed a net a bit further to prevent them from reaching the shore. We're safe."

"You're afraid of sharks?"

"I am, but I hope you're not because I'm about to eat you up alive. I'm aiming for blood tonight, Mags."

All my doubts dissolved at the way Gavin stared at me. Like a predator, he pounded my way, scooped me over his shoulder, and jumped into the water. I laughed with abandon.

"Shhh, we'll attract unwanted attention, Mags." He lowered me to my feet, and with water barely reaching our knees, he kissed me. In a way he hadn't done before. My imagination could easily run wild and imagine this was the way things between us were supposed to be. Now and forever. Because it was simple. Not like anything I'd ever experienced before. My previous long-term relationship had taken a toll on me. Even at its prime, it had never been this easy. This consuming. Or this amazing.

A gruff whimper croaked out and filled the silence. Gavin's mouth searched mine, kissing me until I lost track of time. Of space. Of everything that wasn't us.

One of his hands held my head while the other made its way to the crotch of my bikini bottom. One expert finger slid the thin fabric to the side, pushing inside me. My body quivered against his, my nails digging into the skin of his biceps.

Our eyes met.

Neither of us said anything.

We breathed fast. And shallow.

With every passing second, the tension between us thickened.

When Gavin broke the thick silence, his voice, rough and manly, shattered my restraints to pieces. He could have asked me anything, and I would have agreed. My brain had lost control over my body. The magnetism emanating from the man standing before me was powerful enough to reverse the poles of the Earth. "Bikini off."

I moved to pull the string, but he stopped me. "Not here. What if someone's around."

"We're all alone."

"Not taking any chances. And I don't want anyone else to have access to all that's underneath. I'm pretty possessive of what's mine."

Mine?

In all my life, nobody had ever staked a claim on me the way Gavin just did.

Where was this man all my life?

The one I needed to feel safe. And loved. The one who made me feel special.

At that moment, I never wanted Gavin to ever walk away from me.

Without knowing how he did it, or when, he had seized a chunk of my heart that wasn't for rent. Or for sale. He owned it in the most primal way, and I had no idea what it implied. Only that I liked the feeling of it. No, relished it. This was the way I wanted every single day of my life to be…if love were an option…or if I were seeking it.

Inside the igloo, after he locked the door behind us, Gavin laid me on a massage table. Thanks to our ocean dip, I was dripping wet both on the inside and the outside, my body melting at his sight.

My breathing idled. I gnawed on my bottom lip and watched him, impatient to be sweet-tortured by this man.

"What do we have here?" he asked, rummaging through the paper bag I'd brought from the hotel kitchen. "Chocolate, whipped cream, a bag of ice. Somebody wanted to be bad tonight." A new surge of heat washed through me. Gavin hadn't even touched me, and I was already being consumed by the intensity of his stare.

Tremors rattled my body.

After lighting the candles, each movement deliberate

and purposeful, he removed my bikini slowly. My body sizzled, and his eyes became thirsty abysses I could drown in.

Shudders rippled through me.

"Are you cold?" he asked, his voice rough.

My chest swelled. I craved his hands and mouth on me, ready to worship my needy self.

I shook my head. "I'm so hot, I think I'm gonna melt."

Gavin ran a piece of ice along my lips. I sucked on it, and he tensed. "I'll take care of this." His voice was dripping sex.

I clenched my thighs together, rubbing them to ease the ache building between them.

He twirled the ice cube against my already diamond-hard nipples, hardening them until they hurt. *Please, end me*, I begged in my head. He blew on them, awakening all my senses, then glided the cube lower, still lower, until it reached the apex of my thighs. Flutters awoke under my skin.

Unfiltered desire pooled inside my lower belly.

Gavin positioned himself between my legs. "Are you?"

I nodded. "Clean. On the pill. And about to catch fire if you ignore me any longer. I won't be able to contain the burn. Oh god…"

With one hand, he rubbed the ice cube over my sensitive folds and licked its trail, the warmth of his mouth an addictive contrast to the chilling cold of the ice.

When his tongue entered me, I bit my lower lip as my back arched off the table, unable to process all the euphoria swirling inside me.

My body didn't respond to my commands anymore. It soared from the table, refusing to stay still. The walls of my vagina pulsed. My pummeling heartbeat echoed against the sides of my skull.

Over a candle flame, Gavin melted a chocolate square and used it to draw figures over my naked flesh. Oh. Fucking. God. He devoured me with his tongue, shattering every belief I forced upon me years ago, before pouring rum in the valley between my breasts. The sticky liquid flowed over my stomach, and Gavin licked every drop with his greedy mouth.

Could this be a dream? The word ecstasy now meant something new to me.

All my senses were on high alert. It was the most sensuous thing I'd ever experienced.

Even if I wanted to think—or speak—I couldn't, too busy surfing all those waves of pleasure, Gavin's touch enkindling my cells.

Hovering over me, he branded my body with his tongue. Until he turned me into molten clay and I had no other choice but to let go, bringing him along for the ride.

———

"Mags, why are we on this boat again?"

"Told you already. I'm not telling you where we're going. You wanted me to be a good sport on Christmas Eve a week ago. Now it's your turn. I'm sure we're almost there."

The boat came to a halt, and doubts painted Gavin's face, each shade darker than the previous one.

My smile broadened at the sight of him, noticing every taut line of his face. "You encouraged me to face my Christmas-hatred the other night, and I thought I'd reciprocate. Your—"

"Fuck, Mags. There are sharks encircling us right now," he semi-shouted, scooting further away from the edge of the boat. "I-I…"

Gone was his easy-going attitude. I kneeled before him and grabbed his hands in mine. "As I was saying, we're here to deal with *your* fear."

"How? What-what do you mean?"

"Sharks. And have some fun at the same time. These are Nurse sharks. They're mostly harmless."

Gavin's body went rigid. "No. Not going in there. You said a keyword there. *Mostly.* So yeah, I *mostly* don't wanna get eaten on the last day of the year. I'll pass."

I moved closer and asked, "Do you trust me?"

"Yeah, but I don't trust them," he said pointing to the water.

"It's just you and me out here. We'll pet them. They are like stingrays on steroids."

Gavin lifted both hands, erecting a non-existing wall between us. "I'm not a fan of stingrays either. In fact, ocean creatures give me the creeps."

"Fine," I sighed. "Get comfortable because I'm not missing out on a chance to swim with sharks."

I shimmied out of my shorts and tank top, revealing a black bikini underneath, shaking my ass for good measure. Gavin groaned behind me. The guide gave us a few instructions, and after inhaling a great dose of courage, I entered the water with shaky limbs. In all honesty, I wasn't a fan of sharks either, but when I asked Stella the other day about a private excursion that Gavin and I could do together, she proposed this. I thought it sounded edgy and fun, so I jumped at the opportunity, thinking he might like that.

The curious creatures swam around me.

My chest tightened, and I held my breath, scared that if I made any noise or sudden movements, they would make *me* their end-of-the-year feast.

Could Gavin read the sense of panic invading me? I

hoped not, because I was really doing my best to look brave.

After a long minute, I eased into the shallow, clear-as-crystal waters. For the first time, I admired the scenery surrounding us. The white sand under my feet. The islet on my left, too small to be populated. The azure sky. The beach in the distance. The sight of all this beauty helped me relax. One of the sharks bunted my leg, and I petted his back, smiling at his cat-like antics. I let out a joyous laugh, easing into the experience. My gaze found Gavin's, and I neared the boat, crossing my arms over the rim.

I batted my eyelashes, and he smiled.

"Enjoying your bath with deadly fish?" he asked, mischief in his eyes.

"I would prefer bathing with you, but you know, it's not a prerogative to have fun. If you change your mind, I promise to protect you. It's a once-in-a-lifetime adventure."

Colby, the friendly shark I named after a cartoon, butted my hip this time, and I laughed. "See, even Colby wants you to get in."

"How do you know it's a *he*? Perhaps all your friend wants is to eat us. See? Forget it."

I shrugged. "Fine, I'll let him feel me then. He seems to have a thing for my ass anyway."

"Mags, you're impossible," Gavin said with a loud huff. Without another word, he removed his T-shirt and joined me in the water, a wary look drawn on his face. "I already told you I'm not sharing what's mine."

I looped my arms around his neck, and our lips connected. Colby pushed between us like a jealous child, and Gavin stilled, his eyes fixed on the fish.

"You only came in because Colby has a crush on me. Someone's jealous," I teased.

A guttural bark—one sending my hormones into overdrive—exited his sinful lips. "Mags." My name sounded like a warning when he spoke it.

"Whatever, I'm glad you did. It's safe, okay? You have nothing to worry about."

His heavy intake of air sent a curve to my lips and warmth through my entire being. In the security of each other's embrace, we watched the sharks swimming around us. After a little while, Gavin's rigid stance slackened against me.

"Thanks," he whispered between kisses, "for making me do this. I'm— Ouch, what the hell," he cried, jumping around and letting go of me. He bent over and lifted one foot out of the water. A crab bigger than my hand was clamped to his toe. I pinched my lips together, my shoulders heaving with unshed laughter. I tried to help him, but I was shaking too much with mirth, my movements clumsy. "It hurts, Mags. Stop laughing."

A comedy of errors ensued as all of us—me, the guide, Colby, and the other sharks—moved toward the grown-up man who was hopping in the water, cursing at the crustacean.

The commotion might have confused the crab because, with one kick, it released its prisoner—Gavin's toe—and flew into the boat, landing at our guide's feet.

"Great. You caught dinner." The man smiled proudly, the crustacean dangling between his thumb and forefinger.

I hid my snickers behind my fist, my eyes watering at Gavin's annoyed expression.

"Okay, I'm out of here. The fun has lasted long enough. And no, I'm not eating that for dinner," Gavin said with a sharp tone, lifting himself over the edge of the boat.

That was when I let it all out. Laughter burst out of

me, loud and clear, as tears flowed down my cheeks until the muscles of my sides started cramping painfully.

Gavin glared at me, looking handsome even with that peeved frown fully in place, as more spasms of laughter shook through me.

———

On New Year's Eve, dressed to impress in the glittery red dress that Gavin had gifted me, I threaded through the crowd, a glass of champagne in hand. In my opinion, the New Year's festivities weren't as depressing as Christmas. And the thought of spending the night with the man of my dreams made the decision all too easy.

After our encounter with sharks earlier today, Gavin and I locked ourselves in my room where I proceeded to show him how proud I was that he ventured into the water, by doing all the things he wanted me to. And just for good measure, I did them all over again after a quick nap. I even rewarded him afterward with a shark stuffed animal, that I named Colby, from the gift shop as a token of his courage. Gavin might have said dirty things to me then, igniting my entire being all over again.

Tea and Dolly joined me by the fountain, champagne flutes in hands.

"Dear, you look radiant," the latter said.

"Thanks." A stupid smile grazed my lips, and I was unable to tame it. "Gavin gifted it to me. On Christmas." This time, saying the word out loud didn't make me sick to my stomach. It was as if the mention of that day didn't bother me anymore. Like Gavin had somehow rewritten its meaning in my head. The thought made my grin widen.

"Mr. Gavin has great taste. The dress fits you like a second skin," Tea chimed in.

My pulse danced in a frenzy as I stood there, taking in the man my body and soul recognized as mine, at the bar, deep in a conversation with Gaston.

"Where's Ruth?" I asked, trying to think about anything else but Gavin's lips on mine, his hands on my skin, his manhood taking me to heaven and back, and the way we fit perfectly together.

"She wasn't feeling so well. We urged her to rest. But you know her," Dolly said. "She's upset that she won't be celebrating with all of us tonight."

"Does she need anything?" I asked.

"Nah. Gaston took care of everything." Dolly's eyes darted to the men, still chatting by the bar. Gavin must have sensed the weight of my gaze because he watched me with so much heat I feared my dress might go up in flames. "This man is head over heel in love with you, Maggie. It couldn't be more obvious. Have you two figured out how you'll keep seeing each other once you're back home?" Dolly tapped my hand, while Tea whistled *Oohs* and *Aahs* beside us.

Dolly's words acted as a cold shower.

I only had a few days left at Playa De La Isla Azul.

Then I'd be back in Nashville. And he'd be in Boston.

All week, I'd pushed the depressing thoughts as far as possible every time they crossed my mind, not ready to deal with the reality of our situation. But now, with time running out, the reality of our situation was impossible to ignore.

A strong hand looped around my waist and burning lips connected with the nape of my neck. "You look breathtaking. Sorry if I'm not able to remove my eyes from you tonight, Maggie. You're the most beautiful woman in here. No, scratch that. You're the most beautiful woman I've ever seen." A smile clung to my lips. Gavin had a way of chasing away my fears. Even the deepest ones. "It's almost midnight," his hushed voice spoke against my skin. His presence halted my racing thoughts and, once again, swept me off my feet.

All my cells woke up. Powered by electricity and desire. Pure and unfiltered.

My brain, my body, and my heart all gravitated toward him.

"Wanna do this here or alone somewhere?" he asked, his hand splayed over my stomach as my back faced him. A wave of heat rocked through me. Gavin's words were strong enough to sear my entire self. "This last week, locked in your hotel room, hasn't been quite enough. I need more of you… A whole lot more. I'm still thirsty. And famished. I want to be inside you when the clock strikes midnight."

Were Tea and Dolly right? Were those the words of a man in love?

How could it be? We barely knew each other. Yet a voice in my head I wasn't ready to listen to told me those ladies might have spoken the truth.

Goose bumps blossomed all over my skin.

Waves of panic constricted my chest, crushing all my vital organs.

Warm, unshed tears pooled in my eyes.

Gavin couldn't be in love with me. In all the ways that mattered, I knew he was my perfect match. But still, I wasn't ready to hand him my heart—or to deal with everything that being in love entailed. One day, maybe. Not today, though. Just the thought sent ice down my spine. I didn't want to do love, but I didn't want to let go of him either.

Standing at the edge of the precipice, I didn't know which thought would push me over the edge.

Our time together had an expiration date. And I was unable to return his love—at least not yet. My pulse quickened, and I shook to the marrow of my bones. It hit me. No matter how good we were together or how we longed for each other, this would end. Soon. Too soon. It had to.

The thought alone carved pain into my chest. I would die should it happen. For real. Not just in my head.

My throat worked, swallowing the giant lump lodged inside, and I closed my lids, to chase the sadness away.

I tilted my head back until my cheek rested against Gavin's short stubble, enjoying the rough feel of it on my skin.

I spoke the word that made the most sense, not those burning the tip of my tongue. "Let's stay here."

His body went rigid behind me. "You sure? I was certain you'd want to escape this madness."

I shook my head. "Not this time."

Not ready to show him how vulnerable I felt at the idea of losing him, I spun around and kissed him, preventing him from noticing the tears welling up behind my eyelids in silence.

———

With each passing second of the countdown to midnight, the dread in my chest grew heavier.

The crowd massed around us.

Three...two...one...

Gavin's mouth found mine, and in a lascivious kiss not meant to be witnessed by other people, his lips promised everything I feared. Everything I would run away from. Everything I wasn't ready to face.

He brought both hands to my face, cradling it with tenderness. "Mags, you're the best thing that has happened to me in so long. I don't want to let you go… Not now, not ever… Let's see where this thing between us, this yearning, this thirst for each other takes us, okay?"

I blinked. And blinked again.

My fantasies died, and real life hit me straight in the chest. At full force.

My insides knotted. The weight of the world descended upon my shoulders.

Lava ran in my veins, turning everything to ashes.

No. I couldn't do this. I couldn't promise him we'd be fine. I couldn't promise him forever.

Writhing out of Gavin's embrace, I ran toward the beach, about to collapse without a breath of fresh air. Far from everybody else. Far from where my heart belonged.

"Mags, what's wrong? What did I say? Where are you going? Are you all right?" Gavin asked from behind me. With one turn of my head, I caught the worry swimming in his eyes. He had no right to worry about me—about us. We said casual. We said no strings attached.

All this—the emotions, the connection, the unexpected attachment—was never meant to happen. I wasn't supposed to fall for someone…to have my heart taken hostage.

With my heels hanging from my fingers, I ran further away, past the wellness igloo, until the music from the hotel faded into the distance, replaced by the rhythmic hush of waves crashing against the shore.

"Mags… Wait. Talk to me."

On my knees, careful not to ruin my precious dress, I buried my face in my hands.

Gavin squatted in front of me. "Talk to me. I'm here. I'm not going anywhere. Let me be there for you. Aisha… please."

Why did he have to be so nice? It just made things ten

times harder. If Gavin had been a jerk, I could have tossed him aside without a second thought. But this, he and I, we were in way deeper than I'd ever imagined we would ever be when I propositioned him on Christmas Eve.

"We're over," I cried out, between sobs, avoiding his eyes.

Gavin straightened, and his hands clenched around my thighs.

"Wait. What? What do you mean?" He ran a hand through his hair. "What happened in there?" he asked, pointing to where the hotel stood in the darkness. "I thought we were good… Where is this coming from?"

"Gavin, I want us to break up. Whatever we are, we-we're done. Effective immediately."

He jerked back, then moved to his feet, sending sand scattering with a swift kick. "Stop. You are making no sense right now. Is this a joke? A way to start the new year by messing with me?"

I breathed in some courage and spoke words that felt foreign on my tongue. "This… Us… Celebrating the holidays… The-the New Year. I'm not cut out for this. Long… huh…long-term commitment. At least I'm not ready right now. Hopefully, one day, I-I'll be. But now it's asking too much of me. I'm…I'm sorry. What we shared was fun. We had fun… But it has lasted long enough. Serious relationships freak me out. They need work and time and commitment. And lots of nursing. We said we'd go our separate ways once we went back home. It's for the best. Can't-can't you see it?"

Why were those sentences leaving my mouth? Why was I breaking everything we were with my harsh words? How had my feelings grown so cold that I felt being mean was my only way out of an eminent heartbreak? What was wrong with me?

"You don't mean this… I know you, Mags. It's not you talking, it's your fear. Don't let it win."

"But—"

Gavin dropped his tall self next to me in the cold sand and pulled me into his lap. Only the moon witnessed the fractures of our hearts, the cruelty of my words, and the harshness in my voice. I tried to resist but failed, the battle inside me fading. I had to get the control back. For my sake. And his. Even if I sounded awful right now. Even if I sounded heartless.

I couldn't allow myself to be weak.

"No but. That's what you don't realize. Us together may cure you of your Christmas hatred. Once and for all. And cure me too. A new beginning. You and I. In this together."

I sat upright against his chest and said nothing, looking in the distance, not ready to let Gavin read my deepest thoughts.

"Come on, Aisha… Mags… Or whatever you want me to call you. Let's do this. We owe to ourselves a chance to be happy. To put all our shitty past experiences behind us. I want to try...with you. We are good together. Perfection. What we are can't be faked. It's fucking real. I know it is, and you know it too. I know you do. Even if you're trying to deny it… I'm not buying it."

I wiped my cheeks with a trembling hand.

"Do you trust me?"

I snapped my head to the side as if I'd been struck by lightning. Color must have drained from my face. "Gavin, it has nothing to do with trust. And everything to do with us. We live in different states. We each have our careers. I don't wanna move, and I'm sure you don't wanna leave all those kids in the hands of someone else. I know you… You love them. You care about them. You-you're good with them. You worked hard to get where you are... And so did I."

"I don't agree. We—"

"Don't you see it's better if we parted ways now than wait until life tears us to pieces, just to realize our lives don't fit? For what it's worth, I'll remember these moments we shared forever. And the day I'd be ready to invest myself in a serious relationship, I hope it will make me feel the same way I do when I'm with you. Because you set the bar fucking high, Gavin Moore. You almost make me believe in love again. In happily-ever-afters."

"Don't." Gavin pressed his forehead to the side of my face and brushed my hair with his fingers, his voice cracking. "Why wait? We'll make it work. I'm all in. Whatever it takes, we'll find a way."

"When it ends... It-it always does at some point... It will be too painful and will just increase our dislike for the holidays. It's better if we walk away from each other while we can, instead of waiting for life to rip us apart. Gavin, you made the worst days of the year worth it. You illuminated my world when I lived in darkness, and for that, I'll always be grateful. I don't want to break your heart, but I have no choice. Soon... Soon you'll come to the same conclusion yourself." I moved to my feet, unable to stay still any longer.

"Then don't. Fuck, Mags. Do you hear yourself? You make no sense right now. What are you so scared of? Why can't you have faith we'll make it work? Why? Explain yourself. Be honest with me for once. What did that guy do to you?"

I sniffled, wiping more tears away with my fingertips.

My thundering pulse buried Gavin's protests.

I had it once. The love. The trust. The happy ending. But it was just an illusion back then because it all went up

in flames and squelched my heart until there was nothing
left.

"Mags, say something—"

"I've said my piece." I sniffled. "There's nothing else to
add."

Gavin joined me and clutched my elbow, pleading with
his eyes. The ones I wanted to swim in and forget all about
us drifting apart. My buoy in the storm annihilating my
heart and the heart of the man I cared deeply about.

Chapter 13

Gavin

"What the hell, Mags? Why are you fucking with me right now? Why can't you tell me the whole story just so I understand where you're coming from?" I tried to leash my fury but failed. Big time.

I balled my hands at my side and sent a spray of sand flying in front of me with one kick, trying to make sense of her words.

Aisha steeled her back and held her stand, avoiding my eyes.

"What changed? I thought we got along fine. More than fine. In fact, great. And the sex… Fuck, it's better than anything I've ever experienced before." I relaxed my hands and moved to hug her, the need to protect her, shield her from pain, and heal her heart still burning strong within me.

She recoiled like a startled animal and took a step back.

"What did I do? Or say? I deserve, at the very least, to know why everything changed between us in a matter of hours."

After a beat, she finally spoke the words I feared the most. "I don't want to get attached to you, Gavin. And in all honesty, I could…very easily. I-I…I already am. Everything about you is what I crave in a man…in a relationship. But as I said, I'm not looking for one. Not right now. What I offered you was a no-strings-attached fling. Nothing more. I never thought it would get so deep…so fast. If I had known, how bad this, huh, breakup would be, I…I would've never propositioned you."

I couldn't believe the words spilling from her mouth after I'd been torturing my brain for two days, trying to figure out a way we could still see each other once we were away from here.

"Wow. Do you hear yourself? You would've missed out on us and everything we shared to avoid getting attached? This is ridiculous. You can't just stop caring about me out of the blue because you choose to. It doesn't work like that. You hear me? It's not how it works. Before I met you, I had no clue what the words *chemistry* and *soul mates* even implied. I had no idea I could feel this way. Don't trample on my feelings because of some outdated principle or because you're scared. Stop fighting this. Stop fighting us. Fight *for* us." I paused, inhaling deeply to calm the pressure threatening to burst my chest open. "And who said I wanted to end things?" I asked in a low, controlled voice. "Not me. I wasn't aware this thing between us had a deadline. And I thought we were over that holiday fling deal you proposed. Every time we're together, it doesn't feel like we're just casual… Don't break us up. And don't deny yours the chance to be happy."

Aisha Jones had done some magical voodoo shit on me,

because like a fifteen-year-old in love for the first time, now that I had her in my life, I had no idea how not to be with her after what we experienced over the last two weeks.

I clenched my hands at my sides and closed my eyes. Once I exhaled my wrath out, I opened my eyes to meet her glistening ones.

She had a way to appeal to my emotions. I forgot all about my rage and tightened my grip around her, nestling her against me, right where she belonged. She resisted at first but lost the fight and let go.

"What is it? First, Christmas. Now, this. Tell me the truth. That's all I'm asking."

Aisha wiped her teary eyes on the shoulder of my shirt.

"He did that to me. He made me this way. It's not you… It-it's him. All him. And I hate him even more for that. Gavin, you have to know none of it is your fault."

"Who? What are you talking about? Talk to me, Mags."

With my fingers, I pushed her hair away from her tears-stricken face.

"It happened three years ago. We were getting married. I loved him. And…huh, and I thought he loved me back." She zoned out for a moment, lost in her own thoughts. The desire to pull all the information out of her was strong, but I forced myself to stay calm. *Don't overreact, Gavin*, I repeated in my head. *Whatever she confides in you, don't get upset. And don't kill that motherfucker.*

Aisha continued, drawing me out of my dark thoughts.

"I stood there, at the altar, for forty-five minutes. At first, I thought he had an accident… It had been snowing that day. But-but then my fears transformed into anxiety. And rage. And soon, I wanted to rip his head off." She closed her eyes. "He…He never came. Like an idiot, I waited for him for two hours even after everyone left, hoping he would have a good explanation.... He never showed up. Instead, he flew out of town, forgot all about me, and never bothered to let me know why he freaked out... Why-why he changed his mind. Why he abandoned me there and humiliated me in front of our closest friends and our families."

I held her against my heart, wishing it possessed the power to heal hers. "I'm so sorry. I had no idea. It happened on Christmas day, right?" Aisha nodded, sniffling, her face buried in her hands. "Mags, I would never do that to you. Humiliate you, I mean. Abandon you. You have to know that's not the way I'm wired. All I want is for us to find a way to see each other once we're back into the real world. To be together and give us a chance. We deserve it."

She continued as if lost in her memories once more. "I had that dress, custom-made for me... All white... Looking like something an ice princess would wear, lace, and faux fur at the top and bottom hems. Soft Christmas music was playing as I waited for him to show up. The ceremony and reception were held in a big barn on my aunt's property. All the decor was inspired by a Christmas snow globe. That was the theme. I even had an old engine-red pickup truck with a wreath at the front driving me. A gingerbread house as our wedding cake. A twenty-foot-tall tree had been erected in the middle, with tinsel and hundreds of red and white ornaments hanging from its branches. Underneath it, I had hand-wrapped presents for everyone."

She paused, digging trenches in the sand with her toes.

"Christmas used to be my favorite time of the year. But growing up, I often ended up being on the road or performing during the holidays, so I missed a lot of Christmases with my family. All I wanted was for that night to be special… Not…not only for me, but for everyone else too. To celebrate love. And make up for the years I'd been unable to join the people I cared about, on that day. I wanted Christmas to forever be my special day. To throw the biggest celebration. We had even booked a resort in the snowy mountains for our honeymoon. It-it was supposed to be magical… It was… Instead, I ended up ruining every-one's Christmas that year after they chose to spend the night celebrating me…us…whatever. I can see how selfish I'd been. Wanting it all. But at the time, I really just wished to get married on the most beautiful day of the year, surrounded by my loved ones, and atone for all those missed times…"

Aisha's throat made a bubbly sound. My lips lingered on the crown of her head. She breathed heavily. Every piece of me ached for her, yet my chest swelled with warmth because she had finally opened up to me. "After that day, I loathed every single thing about the holidays. I spiraled into a dark phase for a year… I'm over Carlos. I am. Have been for a long time. But Christmas…Christmas is still a sensitive time in my life. It reminds me of how all my dreams crashed and burned on that day. How I made a fool of myself. How I trusted someone with my heart, and he failed me. How the media never caught a whiff of my mortification, I'm still not sure. Riley, my manager, may have had something to do with it. If they had plastered my humiliation on the front page of some gossip trash, I would have died of shame."

I enveloped her in my arms, resting her against my pounding organ. "I'm so sorry it happened to you. That guy… He's an idiot. Fuck. No wonder you hate Christmas and panicked at dinner the other night. You should have told me. I would've understood." I leaned forward and kissed her lips. "What that loser did to you is unforgivable, but I'm not him. And I'll never be. Christmas isn't him either."

"I know, but you and I…us…it-it got too serious too fast. We're burning steps. Risking my heart isn't an option. I want to trust you… To believe in you. And I know you're nothing like him. But I can't. It's just too much. I'm not ready to put my feelings out there and risk being hurt again."

"We-we can take our time. There's no rush. I just want us to give it a try." Aisha studied me with her red-rimmed eyes. I tipped her chin in my direction when she looked away. "What if we're supposed to be together? You know, the real thing. We're not just a fling. I don't believe it, and you know I'm right. What we share is powerful—and crazy—but it feels right. In a million different ways."

"Gavin, I told you a steady relationship is not what I'm looking for. It's asking too much of me. We made a deal. You knew where I stood when we started this. I'm not ready to invest myself in us…to take that blind leap on trust. I-I have no idea when I'll be… Also, forget about long-distance shit. I'm not convinced it can last in the long run. I've been in the music industry for far too long to know that people rarely stay faithful when they are miles apart, no matter how much they think they love each other…or even if they really do…"

My chest twisted with pain. And so did my stomach. "C'mon, it's bullshit. Many people live this life and have strong marriages. Don't look for flimsy excuses to push me away without giving me a real chance. You're better than this. *We* deserve better than this too."

"Gavin, Carlos not only broke my heart, but he broke everything this period of the year meant to me. He ruined it. Our relationship started on the same day another man got rid of me as if I never mattered to him. This is so wrong. Why can't you see it?"

"So that's it? What we are means nothing to you then? We're just vacation fuck buddies?" The words tasted sour on my tongue. I let go of her, turned around, hiding the pain lacerating my chest. "Fine. Go. Just fucking go. You want to spend your last few days here being alone and miserable, that's up to you. You know how I feel. For what it's worth, I don't agree with anything you said. You're only using these excuses to hide from the truth...from what your heart truly desires. You're a fucking coward. Keep telling yourself all these lies. Go ahead. You're the one hurting yourself. Hurting us… When-when we could be happy… I-I know we could be it. I understand you're scared, but guess what? So am I. You don't see me backing down from taking a chance on us, though. What that jerk did to you was unforgivable. Given a chance, I'd kick his ass to hell. I wish it had never happened to you. Life sucks. Shit happens. So, when that special person is put on your journey, you give them your best, you keep them close, you open your heart fully and completely because that's what relationships—and love—are all about. Besides, this episode of your life has nothing to do with us. You and I, we're the real deal. We're fucking it. I can sense it. Time is no barrier. You said you didn't believe in coincidences. Way to go against your own words. Well played." I paced the deserted beach, unable to calm myself. It was as if my heart's fragile shards were strewn across the shore, lost among seashells, with no way to stitch them back.

"Gavin… I-I'm… Sorry."

"Leave, Aisha. Just leave already," I screamed, spinning around and pointing toward the hotel.

Just a yard from me, the woman leaving me in pieces

gasped. Our gazes locked, but silence hung between us. What else was there to say?

"Goodbye, Aisha," I whispered, struggling against the tightness in my throat once she vanished into the darkness. "I could have fallen in love with you so easily. Fuck, I think I already did." I threw a handful of sand in the water and crumpled on the sandy beach with my face buried in my hands, hating myself for not being enough to hold her back, for not being strong enough to chase away her fears. For not succeeding at showing her what we could be, the two of us. That what we shared was bigger than this world.

An hour later, I watched the waves crash against the shore, scattering seashells, while I drowned my sorrows in a bottle of scotch Vlad gave me a little while ago.

"Happy New Year to me," I hollered, the liquid searing the lining of my throat as I gulped it down straight from the bottle. "What a way to start the year."

The dark ocean, silent and vast, stood as the lone witness to my cries of pain.

Burning tears tumbled down my cheeks. I didn't recall the last time I cried.

After downing more alcohol, I threw the bottle with all my might on the empty beach and passed out on my back, the dancing stars in front of my eyes being the last thing I remembered.

Each of them reminding me of the one I lost.

———

Sunlight blinded me as I cracked open my eyes. Had I really slept all night on the beach? Damn, it was morning already.

I folded an arm over my face.

"Gavin?" For a second, I imagined Aisha changing her

mind and running back to me in her red dress, her hair flowing over her shoulders. The sexy voice closed on me, sounding rougher, and I realized it wasn't even a woman's voice.

I swept my lips with my tongue and before rubbing against my upper teeth, trying to chase away the pasty taste in my mouth. In vain.

With a kink in my neck and knots in my back, I adjusted my wrinkled shirt and sat with my arms draped around my bent knees.

"Gavin. Son, are you all right?" Gaston asked from my right. I raked my fingers through my hair, trying to comb it back in place. I sighed. I must have looked like shit.

"Yes. No. Not even close," I said, my feelings about to spill out of me through every pore. "She broke it off. Aish…Maggie… She got scared and dumped me. As if I never mattered to her. Nothing. Fuck it." I shook my head. "All because she's afraid of what we could be…of love and getting her heart broken." I punched the sand between my legs. "What a fucking amazing first day into the new year."

Gaston sat beside me. "You know, son. Women are complicated beings. Ruth and I have been together a long time, but it hasn't always been easy. Back in the day, she didn't make it easy on me." He linked his hands together, his head tilted forward, lost in old memories. "The moment I saw her, I knew I'd spend the rest of my life with her…no matter how long it would take me to prove her wrong. And believe me, she resisted my charms for quite some time. I didn't let it dissuade me, though. We had the same group of friends, so we were always around each other. One day, another guy broke her heart, and I was there to comfort her. From that day on, we spent most of our free time together, without our friends, and one night, in my pickup truck, she kissed me. The kiss I had been longing for my entire life. After that, I didn't have to convince her anymore that we were destined to be together. She sensed it. That kiss sealed the deal."

I rubbed the heels of my hands over my burning eyes. "We already kissed…many times. And they've all been pretty perfect. In every way. But she doesn't want to commit. Nothing I'll do or say will change her mind. It's not like I can barge into her life and force her to see things my way. She made it pretty clear she wants to be left alone."

"Sometimes women need to face what they're missing to realize what they want. You and Maggie remind me of Ruth and I. Soul mates. That thing between you guys is powerful… No wonder she panicked. Ruth told me on our twentieth wedding anniversary that she had loved me for a long time before we started dating but was too afraid that the attraction, strong and heady, between us would lead to heartbreak. So, she fought against it for as long as she could until she had exhausted all excuses to run from what her heart wanted."

I shook my head, sieving sand between my fingers. "What do I do now?"

Gaston clapped my shoulder. "Figure out what *you* want. Far from here. When you're back in your everyday life. And if Aisha is still the one, then fight for her. With everything you have. You two deserve to be happy. With or without each other. Believe an old man or not, but I'm certain things will turn out okay. Aisha Jones is in love with you, son. Whether she knows it or not. Give her some time to adjust to the idea and to miss you."

Aisha Jones is in love with you, son. Whether she knows it or not. Give her some time to adjust to the idea and to miss you.

Deep down, I knew Gaston's words made sense. Even if I had no idea what I should do about it. My crushed heart trembled inside my chest. How could I prove to her we were the real deal?

Reality hit me, and I angled my body toward the wise man sitting beside me. "How did you know?"

A wide smile brightened his face. "Son, we've known from the beginning. The four of us might be old, but we're not stupid. We do listen to her music."

"Still, none of you said anything."

"If Ms. Jones came to this island to spend her vacation in peace, wanting her privacy, then she didn't need to be greeted by groupies. For us, she's just a nice woman you met. Nothing more. Nothing less. It's evident she enjoys the anonymity and has some baggage she needs to deal with. And we all love how down to earth she is, not using her fame to coerce people to like her or request special treatments." Gaston, balancing himself with a hand on my upper arm for support, slowly moved to his feet. "For what it's worth, I wish you luck, son. Not that you need it, though." He winked. Yep, the old man winked at me. "Maybe we'll see the two of you again next Christmas. Who knows? We're leaving tomorrow. Why don't you join us for dinner tonight? Ruth and the girls would love to spend one more night with you. Unless you prefer being left alone, crying into your pillow."

"I-I…"

"Think about it." He spun around and walked away.

For the next hour, I stayed put, my ass glued to the sand, as the beach buzzed around me, filled with the joyous sounds of people celebrating the New Year. Gaston's words replayed in my head as I tried to put some order into my thoughts.

And my heart.

Chapter 14

Aisha

A knock on the door startled me. "I'm not here," I shouted, placing a pillow over my head, silencing the sobs that had been rocking my body since last night.

A part of me had been wishing the whole time that Gavin would barge in here and heal the broken pieces of me by kissing me, forcing me to give us a chance and not freak out so much.

He never did.

I'd been locked in my room all day, too scared that I'd run into him. In case that my heart snitched on me, giving away how much I cared and how badly I wanted to give us a real shot.

That knock again. *Come on, let me grieve in peace.*

The slim chance it could be Gavin after all brought me to my feet.

I firmed my back, and after smoothing my shirt with my fingers, I pried the door open.

"*Ho, ho, ho*, Ms. Jones," cheered Stella, a Santa hat on her head and a huge smile pasted to her lips. Didn't she get the memo Christmas was over more than a week ago? Oh yes, Las Palmeras was a year-long themed resort. How could I forget? She handed me a bag. "All your clothes and other belongings. From Domingo Resort. Everything has been cleaned. They'll reach out within a week or two to settle the claim for the unsalvageable items. I hope you had a great time with us."

I nodded. My eyes were probably bloodshot and swollen. No doubt I looked a mess. Even then, the woman's cheerful grin didn't faze.

"If you need anything before you go, come and find me."

I shook my head, unable to hide the dumbfounded look on my face.

I dried my watery eyes with my sleeves. "I'm sorry, Stella. Th-thank you. This is… This is painful. Being heartbroken. I thought he would run after me… He didn't. But I didn't want him to, right? Even though I pushed him away and said hurtful things to him. How could he have known it was my fears talking? But he did… I was the one who insisted it wasn't. Ohmygod, I'm not making any sense right now. Thanks… Thank you for bringing my stuff. You could have kept it, you know. Everything in this room will forever remind me of him. Of what I've lost. Because…huh, I'm sad. Please tell me I'm stupid and I should go after him. No. Don't. We can't happen. I have too much stuff I need to figure out. Did you ever meet someone you thought had been put on this Earth with the sole purpose to care for you, love you, steal your heart? Again, don't answer. Every bit of me yearns for him. I…I swear. It's my head that's not ready. There's too much at stake… It's irrational… I-I'm being irrational."

Stella squeezed my forearm. "Ms. Jones, it will get better."

I sniffled. "You think? I hope so. Or I will never recover from this. I'll be screwed up for the rest of my life. Again, I'm sorry for dumping my sorrows on you. I have no one to talk to. He has friends here. I-I have nobody. Once again, I'm all… Ohmygod, I'm all alone…and hurting. This time, it's all my fault. I'm the one to blame."

I stepped forward and wrapped my arms around her.

Gosh, she must think I'm wasted. Or crazy.

"Thanks for listening to me vent. I know I make no sense to you." I sighed and took a step back, adjusting my shirt.

Stella offered me a soft smile.

"Ms. Jones. Put a dress on and enjoy your last day on our island. The sun will be good for you. See me in an hour; I'll book you a massage. You'll like that."

I nodded. "Yes," I said through sobs, the curtain of tears blurring my vision. "Thank you. Again, sorry for unloading all this on…on you."

Stella left, and I stood there, unable to move.

She was right, though. Things would get better. Once I returned home. I had a new album coming out in a few months. That would take my mind off things.

I grabbed my phone and sent Riley a message.

ME

> It's me. Hope you had fun in New York. Please tell me you got me lots of studio time next week. Can't wait to dive into this new album. I'll be home soon.

He replied within a minute.

RILEY

> Glad to hear it. The studio has been booked for months. Ready to start. Thought Carter could join you on "Lost and Found." Make it a duet. Let me know if you like the idea. Have a safe flight back and talk to you soon, kiddo.

All the worries rushing in me settled.

This was my life.

Tomorrow night I would be back home, doing what I was born to do, and this vacation would only be a bittersweet memory from the past.

I showered, changed, and went downstairs to take Stella up on her offer for a massage.

———

I felt him before I could see him—Gavin—busy talking with a man by the giant Christmas tree in the hotel lobby.

Our eyes met for a half-second before I averted mine, unable to deal with the pain overflowing from his.

I put my shades on and heard the words, "Goodbye, beautiful star," drowned out by the crowded lobby as I sauntered toward the shuttle parked outside that would take me to the airport. In the far back, I sat with my head pressed against the window, earbuds on, and let music soothe my broken heart. And my soul.

Eight hours later, I entered my home, drained, my feelings still crushed and hurting.

With a cup of tea in hand, I watched the snowflakes through the den window, missing the shining stars that had brightened my nights for the last two weeks.

Even at this late hour, I shot Riley a message.

ME

Home. Don't reply. Just wanted to let you know.

Then I sent one to my mother.

ME

Back in town. I'll come see you tomorrow. I love you.

MOM

Can't wait to hear about your trip. I missed you.

Memories of Carlos, the man who wounded me years ago, resurfaced.

I knew I had to deal with them. Once and for all. I couldn't let his betrayal control my life any longer. My misery had dragged on long enough. This time I would make sure I healed. For real.

How can I love Gavin with everything I am if I'm not capable of loving myself fully? Or something as merry and peaceful as Christmas?

The bouts of crying and the way every corner of my being ached for Gavin—something I'd never experienced before—had shown me how wrong I'd been to push him away. Even if I still believed our relationship had gotten too intense too fast, I wasn't ready to risk my heart. Not until I pieced the broken parts of it back together.

A fat tear glided down my cheek, and I caught it with my fingertips.

I blinked, strangled sobs erupting from the depths of me and piercing the silence of my home, the snowflakes outside witnessing the extent of the hurt coursing through me. And the bottomless pit of pain I was in.

The tears now ran freely down my face, washing the bruises of my scarred heart.

After a moment, I dried my watery eyes with a tissue, sniffling, then inhaling a few healing breaths, doing my best to put to rest the emotional storm raging inside me.

How did Gavin succeed in making me long for things I thought I was not ready for in life in so little time?

How did he weave himself into my soul like no one else ever had before?

How did he touch my soul in the deepest way with only a look, a heartfelt smile, or a caress of his lips?

I brought my hot beverage to my lips, savoring the warmth as it slid down, leaving a comforting trail behind.

I cleared my throat, strangling the mug between my hands to prevent the tremors. "Gavin… I-I'm sorry I wasn't ready for you. It will forever be my biggest regret. I wish you happiness. Loads of it. Because you're entitled to the best. You're the most amazing person I've ever met, and I wish I could have been ready to love you too."

I blinked the remnants of my tears away, drawing from deep within me the strength to calm my pounding heart.

After a moment, I sat at the piano and placed my mug on top.

My fingers skimmed the white keys, and the simple contact eased their trembling. Music had always been my escape. My way of dealing when too many emotions suffocated me, and I had no idea how to cope with them.

I played the first notes of "Better Now," a ballad from my latest album that I co-wrote and that served as a form of therapy for me back then.

My voice, hoarse from days of tears, carried the first verse. I coughed a little, releasing the tension around my vocal cords.

The world around me stopped existing. I forgot all

about my heartbreak as the words flew out my mouth. I kept my eyes closed, experiencing the vibration of each note through my body.

> **I know, this wasn't supposed**
> **to go down this way**
> **I was waiting, you shouldn't**
> **have left that day**
> **Oh, why did I let you stomp on**
> **my heart?**
> **Now you're gone, and I can**
> **finally breathe on my own**

My second hand joined in, and I lost myself in my art, attacking the chorus, my lids sealed, my voice steadier.

> **I'm better on my own.**
> **Stronger, fiercer, wiser**
> **I'm better on my own. Free,**
> **happy, lively**
> **Boy, I'm not settling for less**
> **than I deserve**
> **Everything is better now, I'm**
> **moving forward**
> **I'll show you and everybody**
> **else what I'm made of**
> **Watch and see, boy**
> **You thought I wasn't good**
> **enough for you**
> **But it's you who's not good**
> **enough for me**
> **(Yeah) You'll be sorry when**
> **you see me shine in the sky**

With a new resolve and the desire to take my life back into my own hands, I went to bed. Wanting to close the doors to my past forever, I found myself, for once, eager about the new year ahead. Though losing Gavin would always be the splinter that would never allow my heart to become whole again.

When I woke up the next morning, the pain of the heartbreak still lingered deep inside me, but music found its way back to my soul. My groove was back. Or some of it was, at least. I wouldn't give myself any time to wallow and let *what-ifs* creep in. I could be strong. I had to be. I puffed my chest out, tied my hair in a top-knot, and pushed my sleeves up, ready to face the day.

"Yeah, let's do this, girl."

Chapter 15

Aisha

Eight days later, I greeted Carter Hills as he walked into the small studio that had been mine for the last three days.

"I'm happy Ry called me. Love the song. I think it will be a hit. And you know I'm always right about these things."

"Got the lines you changed," I said. "It sounds way better. I should always ask you two to write my songs for now on. Tell April she did a good job on 'That Summer' and 'I'm a woman.' I love her songwriting. She understands how I think… Or what's in my head."

Carter's laughter vibrated through me. "You can tell her yourself. She's in town with me. We're having dinner with Ry and Devon later. You should join us."

Another part of my heart healed. I had great people around me. Wonderful people. I wasn't so alone after all.

"I'd like that. Ready?"

"Yeah, let's do this," Carter said, taking his guitar out of the case.

An hour later, we sat by the console, listening to the song we just recorded. It sounded great. No, more than great. It sounded amazing. Wonderful. Perfect.

Silent tears streamed down my cheeks when the chorus started.

**We were lost. We were alone.
But life brought us
together.
We were lost. We were sad. But
it's over 'cause we belong
together.**

Carter draped his strong arm around my heaving shoulders.

"It's okay," he whispered.

I shook my head. "No, it's not."

Soon my words were drowned by my sobs.

———

That night, the five of us sat in one of my favorite restaurants located atop a commercial high-rise in downtown Nashville.

Riley raised his glass after the server poured each of us some wine. "To you guys. You're my family in more ways than you'll ever know. I can't wait for our entire group to be reunited again. I wish Sam, Dahlia, and Stud were here with us tonight."

We all cheered to that.

"How was the vacation, Aisha?" April asked.

Devon chimed in. "Yeah. I heard great things about Playa De La Isla Azul. Riley is not really a *basking in the sun* type of a man, but I thought we could give it a try later this year."

I swallowed hard. "The island is magnificent. Domingo Resort was great…for the one day it lasted."

I scolded myself and took a long drink of wine. Why did I open my stupid mouth? I knew my country family. They wouldn't pass up a chance to tease me about my misfortune.

I huffed when Carter asked, "A day? I thought you spent two weeks there."

"Someone hung Christmas lights to the sprinkler heads, and that set it off. In the middle of the night, my room turned into a river. They moved me to another hotel because Domingo Resort had no vacancy… I ended up in a…huh…never mind." Emotions swirled inside me, and I bit back my tears as memories of my vacation hit me. I was still not ready to deal with them. I thought I was. I really did. But now I wondered if I would ever be.

"Come on. Continue," Devon encouraged me. "Why do I feel the crunchy part of your story is coming up? Girl, you can't end it there. We need to know the rest."

"She's right, Aisha," April added, patting my hand. "I'm curious to know the story too. It's us. Riley said it first, but I agree, we're family."

I downed half of my wine and shook my head. "Nah. It's boring, anyway. How are the kids?"

Riley cleared his throat, and we all knew what it implied. "Kiddo, we all have embarrassing stories. You've heard them. We could write a series just from our Carter Hills Band days. Oh god, it was a whirlwind of a time."

Carter let out a low whistle, followed by a quiet chuckle. "See, we've all been there. Part of the job. Don't be shy."

"I'm not shy," I protested, not meeting his eyes.

"So, what is it? Did something happen?" My manager shifted in his chair, leaning forward from the other side of the table, searching my eyes. "Aisha Jones. You told me you were fine. I knew Scooter should have gone with you. Never again you're going on a vacation by yourself. It's not like you were there with friends who had your back. Scooter is your security detail, and from now on, he goes where you go even when you don't agree. Don't attempt another vanishing act on your own. And the matter is not open for discussion."

"I—"

"No, it's settled, Aisha. Now tell me who messed with you on that trip."

Riley Burns had his *I'm not fucking kidding* face on. The one he only wore while talking business.

The emotions I'd kept carefully leashed inside threatened to burst out.

How could I let myself believe I was doing better? That I was over Gavin?

I closed my eyes to draw in a long breath and fidgeted with the stem of my glass.

All my friends' eyes darted to me.

Deep down, I knew they meant well. But I didn't find it easy to confide in them about my wreck of a love life. Or the one I lost, not because I didn't care, but because I didn't hold on when it mattered most. They were all blissfully happy, and here I was, all mixed up in the strings of my emotions and unable to follow my deepest desires, even though I knew they were right.

Beside me, Devon squeezed my hand. "Aisha, did someone hurt you?"

Before dating Riley, the woman had endured years of physical abuse. I refused to let her think I went through something as traumatic.

The only thing broken in me was my heart… or maybe my sanity, because I let Gavin walk away without fighting for us, just as he had asked. Despite him being nothing but selfless, protective, and caring toward me.

Meeting her eyes, I shook my head. "Nobody hurt me," I muttered in a low voice. "I hurt myself...all on my own."

"What do you mean?" Carter asked, his expression serious as he studied me.

I took a deep breath in, hoping seeds of courage would grow inside me. "Okay, fine. You're not allowed to laugh. You're not allowed to say *I told you so* or whatever shit my mother would say." They all nodded, their eyes round and full of anticipation. "They shipped me to an all-year-round Christmas-themed resort, and I had to wear candy-caned patterned clothes because my luggage was ruined and had to be left behind, and I was offered melted Santa cocktails at the bar. People wore Santa hats instead of baseball caps, and *elf* shoes." Someone gasped, but I looked down, not willing to see the stares on me. "But then something happened. I met this guy… Gavin. He took me shopping when I had nothing but ridiculous outfits to wear. We clicked. He cared for me... He truly cared about me… And he helped me get through the two weeks…" My voice cracked on the last word as more emotions battled inside me.

"And?" April's soft voice acted as a protective blanket over my wounded heart.

"He gifted me the most beautiful dress." My throat tightened as my pulse thundered inside my chest. "He was amazing."

"Where is he now? Are you two dating?" Devon asked.

I motioned no with my head. "Things got serious, like really serious, really fast, and I pushed him away. On New Year's night... After he... Oh gosh, I-I can't believe I did that. I pushed him away after he opened his heart to me and told me we should keep seeing each other when our vacation was over. He said we were the real deal." I exhaled. "I panicked. And...and I never talked to him again after that night. Not my proudest moment."

April leaned closer. "Why?"

I shrugged. "Because. How can we make it work? We don't really know each other... And we're different. He lives in Boston. I live here. He's an art therapist with kids on the autism spectrum. Painting. Music. All this stuff. I'm going on a world tour next summer. Our lives do not blend... And I'm not looking for a relationship so..."

Carter nudged his wife, and they exchanged a glance. Yeah, they'd been there too. When they first met.

"Aisha—" I lifted my head to eye my manager. "Why didn't you call? Or text? I would have gotten you out of there. We all know how Christmas is a sour topic in your life."

Devon slapped his arm. "No. Stop trying to play the hero here. Did you not hear a word she said? She fell in love while she was there. It wouldn't have happened if she had stayed at Domingo Resort. I love you, but mind your own business for once. Their love story is like a Christmas fairytale. Don't get involved."

My manager raised both his hands in surrender. "Sorry, Dev. I just wanted to help."

She leaned toward him, and their lips met. I looked away. "I know. Your heart is huge. That's why I love you so much." They kissed a little more.

"What now?" April asked.

"Nothing. He's back in Boston"—I shrugged—"and I'm here. We never even exchanged phone numbers. It's better this way. Let's just call it a vacation hookup. A Christmas story. Not all tales have a happily-ever-after ending. Now I need to move on. To get back up there. Finish my album. Get ready for the tour. Do the things I love the most and enjoy every minute of it. I'll get over him. One day… I have to."

Was I trying to convince them or myself?

I wiped the unshed tears prickling my eyes with my napkin.

My friend moved to her feet and wrapped her arms around me. "You know you don't have to choose between what you want and what is expected, right? Or let your reasons win over your emotions. I've been in your shoes. Scared. Afraid to commit. And I ran away. But soon I realized my life made no sense if my heart was unhappy. Luckily, Carter fought for me…for us. He never lost faith in us. Even after I left him and refused to marry him the first time, even after he opened his heart and showed me his vulnerable side."

Fresh tears built in my eyes, and I let out a little laugh. "Sorry."

April squeezed my forearm and sat back. "It's okay. We all do stupid shit when our hearts' desires clash with our brain's common sense. It's absurd. We drive ourselves nuts when we try to control all variables. Look at Carter and me now. We're lucky we found each other…even if the timing seemed wrong at that time. Even if, from an outsider's point of view, we moved too fast. Still, we embarked on a whirlwind romance after just weeks of knowing each other, and it turned out to be the most sensible thing either of us has ever done. And Devon moved in with Riley the second time they saw each other. Sure, there's a backstory, but they made it work."

I sniffled and smiled through my tears. "I know you're right. What if it's too late, though? I said awful things to him the last time we talked. Things I regret deeply and can't take back. He was all sweet and amazing as usual, and I blew him off. Big time. I broke his heart and stomped on it with both feet. Huh, to-to make sure he would never want to be with me again. I sabotaged everything we could have been."

Riley shifted on his chair to face me. "If you could have anything, what would you wish for, kiddo?" he asked.

"Him. I'm sad since we parted ways. My heart has stayed behind on that island," I confessed with a sigh. "Truthfully, I need Gavin in my life. His light, his humor, his affection…his love. Everything about him is amazing. He makes me a better person. I feel like myself when he's around. He's perfect for me. I'm not afraid when he holds my hand. His touch alone is enough to kill all the doubts swirling in me. And when he stares at me, I feel alive. And strong. And beautiful. I wonder how it's even possible he exists and checks all the boxes on my perfect-guy list."

Sitting on each side of me, April gasped, and Devon clapped her hands.

"I have an idea," the latter said. "Go freshen up, I'll order shots. You need to have a little fun and let go for a night. Tomorrow you'll think about a strategy to win your man back. I'll even come over to brainstorm if you need my help. Coincidences do not exist, Aisha. Don't you see? Life brought you two together. Or maybe Santa did," she said with a wink. "You know, Christmas magic and all. Everything that occurred on that trip brought you to him. I don't believe it was luck. Life gifted you the man of your dreams because you deserve him. People would kill for a chance like that. You owe it to yourself to see where it will take you. Don't waste time asking yourself why, just go for it if he's the one you can see yourself going the distance with."

More tears clouded my vision. My girlfriend's words dashed straight to my heart. "Thanks."

Minutes later, I exited the ladies' room, and from a distance, I studied my friends. April sat on her husband's lap, her arms looped around his neck, whispering in his ear. The way his hand gripped her thigh and they grinned at each other; I could only imagine what it was about.

Riley stood behind his ladylove, his hands resting on her shoulders, leaning forward to kiss her, upside down.

My insides crackled with emotion.

I had that.

The chemistry. The love. The passion.

Love? Could it be? Ohmygod, could I be in love? The reality of those words I feared for a long time hit me. Yeah. I loved Gavin Moore. I really did. Now everything made sense. As if I'd just elucidated my life's biggest mystery. *Love.* Wow. That explained why leaving Gavin behind had hurt so fucking much. Why, no matter what I did, I felt like a chunk of my heart had gone missing, a part of me had never returned, and a major source of happiness in my life had run dry.

The lyrics of "Lost and Found," Carter's and my song, replayed in my head.

> **We were lost. We were alone.**
> **But life brought us**
> **together.**
> **We were lost. We were sad. But**
> **it's over 'cause we belong**
> **together.**

I joined my friends at our table, and my good mood returned. Sure, my vital organ trembled behind my ribs at the idea of listening to its wishes and going after Gavin hoping he'd agree to give me a chance.

Carter and Riley pulled me aside just as I was about to leave the restaurant.

Riley spoke first. "Aisha, if that man of yours comes back into your life, and I'm pretty sure he will—he'd be crazy to let you go—well, we want to meet with him."

My eyes traveled between both men.

"You said he was an art therapist, right?" Riley asked.

I shrugged. "Yeah. So, what about it?"

Carter'expression grew serious. "You know the foundation April and I started to help children and teens reach their full artistic potential? We've been thinking about expanding it to kids with special needs. Their talents deserve to be recognized too. Riley has been helping me find the right person to set it up but so far, we haven't been successful. It takes great skills to work with those kids so that they thrive the way they should. We're looking for someone passionate. Someone who will give all they have for those kids."

"Ohmygod, Gavin would be perfect," I whispered.

"Yes. You mentioned his career, and it just clicked. Call it a hunch, but something inside me told me he'd be a great asset to what we're building. We're not only looking for someone to help around but for someone to handle and manage that side of the foundation. Who knows, maybe he would be interested to discuss it. The person in charge will have funding, and we'll provide them with everything they need to run it smoothly. If you ever hear from him again, please connect us. If it's not asking too much."

"You're serious?" Carter nodded. "Gavin lost part of his funding before the holidays and was devastated. I'm sure he'd want to hear what you guys have to say. He's fond of those kids. He'd work *pro bono* if it means providing every one of them with services adapted to their needs. Whatever happens between us, you have to meet with him. You're right; I'm sure you guys would be a great fit. I'll let you know how it goes. And Ry, I may need some help to track him down. Your connections are always better than mine."

I winked, and he winked back before dropping a kiss at the top of my head.

"Go get some rest, kiddo. We'll talk later. We have your back. All of us."

After I hugged April and Devon, I hauled myself into the backseat of a cab, my thoughts drifting to times gone by…and Carlos. I shook my head as the silent words in my mind spoke the truth for the first time.

Why did you leave me there? At the altar? By myself? You could have been honest with me. I'm sure I would've understood. I thought you loved me… You didn't. I thought I loved you… I'm not sure anymore. You know, I've met someone… Someone great. Someone who wouldn't have left me at the altar on Christmas day. I wish I had met him instead of you that morning in that coffee shop. Things would have been different if I had… So much better. I wouldn't have run away from things that used to make me happy if I had. All this time I thought I hated Christmas, but now I understand what the people I love have been trying to drill into my brain for years. It's not Christmas I hate, it's you. No, not you, but how you made me feel. Like I didn't count… Christmas time is a painful reminder of the humiliation you put me through that day. I'm done suffering. All I want is to enjoy life, not dwell on the past. I shouldn't be scared to trust someone else with my heart, yet I am. I've never said those words to you, Carlos, but go to hell. I should have told you the day you came over to pick up your stuff. In hindsight, with a bit of introspection…

thank you for setting me free and showing me that I deserve better. You were never worth the tears I cried.

Calm seeped through me, as if speaking the words had erased the chains around my heart. It felt free and light for the first time in many years. And excited at the idea of seeing the man it belonged to. Again. And hopefully forever.

Wishing he would still have me. Even after everything.

Chapter 16

Gavin

I emptied my lungs in one big huff, my messenger bag slung across my body and my hands shoved in the pockets of my jeans as I entered the room hosting my painting group-therapy session. Some of the kids cocked their heads to acknowledge me, but most didn't. I bit back a smile. Yep, I loved these kids.

Our offices were located in a dead-end street, far from the noises of the city. We had a large yard for the kids to play, with swings and slides.

Inside were the offices of many specialists, including psychologists and other therapists. The painting room had large windows on one side, offering a view of the garden, and a darker corner on the other side, for kids sensitive to light or other sensory issues and those preferring working in semi-darkness or using colorful light beams.

Everything was neatly arranged around the room.

The kids always occupied the same stations, each of

them working on their own, focusing on their pieces of art, barely ever interacting with one another.

I stowed my bag in my assigned space near the door and scanned the room. Beverly was already deep into her painting activity, the three-by-four canvas before her filled with precise brush strokes. This month, her colors of choice were blue and yellow. Last month, it was red and orange. She never mixed her colors—even when she painted. She always made sure the previous coat had dried enough before applying a new color. The nine-year-old was skilled. Like ridiculously skilled. A few months back, I even got a local gallery to showcase two of her artworks.

Craig Kauffman neared me and offered me a handshake. "You sure you're ready for this?" he asked.

My eyes traveled around the room. No. How could I ever be ready? A tightness grew inside my chest. My eyes prickled. No doubt this would be the hardest thing I would ever do. But I knew it was for the greater good. These kids deserved the best in life, and I would make sure they got it. Every single one of them. And all the other ones too.

I swallowed hard, sadness stacking higher with every breath.

Yesterday, I had to say goodbye to my music class. Just the memory of it was enough to trigger an avalanche of emotions inside me. I breathed in and pushed them down. I could deal with them later.

"Look how they're thriving. I'll do everything I can to make sure more kids like them have that chance."

Craig clapped my shoulders and offered me a warm smile. "Moore, you're one of a kind."

I nodded and said nothing because my throat clamped, and I swallowed the new wave of emotion trying to burst out.

A loud cry followed by the sound of an easel hitting the floor cut our discussion short.

Beverly pressed both hands to her ears and rocked her body back and forth, screaming and kicking.

Craig motioned to join her, but I clutched his elbow to stop him. "Please, let me."

Cynthia, our newest intern, looked at me with wide eyes.

"What happened?" I asked her.

"Carl tripped over his feet and bumped her chair. She dipped the brush meant for the blue paint into the yellow one."

"Oh. Okay, I'll take it from here."

Next to Beverly, I sat on a little plastic chair, two feet from her. I knew the girl liked her bubble big around her. And that she never mixed things. Not her food and even less, her paint. And also, she never dirtied her fingers. Now she had blue paint all over the side of her hand, and her colors had been mixed together.

"Beverly, we can fix this. We'll get you new paint with new brushes. It's okay." I put the easel back on its feet and leaned forward with paper towels in my hands, ready to clean the mess on the floor when an idea hit me. I took a new sheet of paper from the stack on the table behind me and used the mixed paint to trace green patterns. Beverly froze, eyeing me with interest. Her kicking and screaming stopped.

A soft laugh exited her mouth, and a wave of emotion rose within me.

After a minute, she stole the paintbrush from my hand and traced more patterns on the sheet.

"Look, you've created green paint. It's pretty cool, right?"

Without a word, the little girl used the newly-mixed

color as I refilled her palette with fresh paint after washing it.

"You're doing a great job, Beverly. If you want to make new shades of colors, come see me today, I'll show you how."

She glanced at me sideways but said nothing, her focus now back on her two-colored project.

I finished cleaning the mess at her feet and joined TJ who was painting by numbers at a low table in a dim-lit corner of the room. TJ had made lots of progress in the last three months. He loved baking, and every day he came here, we ate our snack together as I tried his latest cookie recipe. Today was oatmeal and pumpkin spice.

Twisting a fidget tangle between his fingers, TJ met my eyes, something that he'd been doing a lot more lately. His social skills had improved tremendously with the group sessions. Most kids ignored each other, but the fact that they had to share the space and be around other children could be a challenge. So far, it had been beneficial for many of them. TJ's father told me the other day the pediatrician had been impressed at his last visit, when his son answered some questions by himself.

"TJ," I began, knowing how important it was to explain changes to kids on the spectrum. Most of them loved defined boundaries and things a certain way. Being honest with them about anything new coming up lessened part of their anxiety and helped them prepare for what was about to come. "I need to tell you something. You know I told you the other day I would be going on a trip? To help more kids?" He nodded, pushing a piece of cookie into his mouth. "Today is my last day here. Craig will be working with you from now on. You know Craig. His jokes are lame, but don't tell him I said that." A hint of a smile grazed TJ's lips. "I brought cake today, and we'll have a little party later. I just wanted you to know."

"Cake?"

"Yes. And juice boxes. Your dad will be here too. I hope it's okay with you." TJ nodded, and his eyes darted back to his work-in-progress. "I'll let you finish this. Thanks for the cookie. I can't decide which one is my favorite. I'll miss sampling your recipes."

The boy offered me a lopsided smile, his gaze meeting mine for a split second.

Before I could leave, he jumped to his feet and wrapped his arms around me.

I fought back a wave of tears.

TJ's squeeze tightened around me, and my hand ruffled his ginger hair.

"I'll miss you too, TJ. You'll always hold a special place in my heart."

A guttural sound caught my attention. Behind us stood Cole. At six-foot-three, two-hundred-fifty pounds, wearing a permanent frown, the fifteen-year-old looked imposing— and somehow threatening. Until you noticed Mathilda, his favorite doll, hanging from one hand. Then he looked more like a gentle giant with a scowl, lost in a body too big for him.

Cole didn't talk. Never. He only growled.

With his head tilted forward, he glared in my direction, his stare not meeting mine.

The boy had a talent for drawing. He only drew eyes, though. Humans. Animals. Any kind of eyes. With char-coal. In the entire group, he and Beverly had the most impressive artistic gifts.

The other kids used the arts mostly to communicate and express themselves. But these two were amazing to watch as if their entire worlds only opened up when they faced a blank canvas.

TJ let go of me and returned to his art project.

Cole stood there, immobile, watching me, his head cocked to the side.

"You want a hug too, Cole?" I asked. The teen never showed affection to anybody except his precious doll—the one his big sister gifted him when they were small kids.

I let my arms fall to my side as I waited. Another growl left his mouth, and he started rocking on his heels. Just when I thought he would go back to his drawing, he pounded in my direction, looped his big arms around my shoulders— we were about the same height, but the kid had a good fifty pounds on me, and he had shoulders twice the width of mine—and squeezed so hard, my feet lifted from the floor.

At that moment, I couldn't hold back the swirl of feelings rushing inside me anymore. The tears I had been locking in for the last few weeks flowed out.

This. This was the highlight of my career. Having Cole show another person affection in the purest way—something his parents had come to terms with a long time ago when he was still a child and screamed every time they tried to hug him. Having Cole tell me he'd miss me like I'd miss him. With his display of affection, he showed me my work wasn't in vain. That it meant something. It helped those kids. I mattered to them. It hit me, and just like that, the dam inside me gave way, releasing a flood of tears.

"I love you too, Cole. And I'll miss you. A lot. I'll come back to see you. I'm so proud of you. You're doing great."

After a few minutes, his grip on me lessened, and without a word or a look in my direction again, the kid went back to his drawing, slouching on the same yellow bean bag kept in a corner, that he used every time he came here, where streams of changing lights illuminated the walls and surfaces.

I scanned the room, and an unfamiliar pain coursed through me. The pain of leaving but knowing it was for all the good reasons.

The rest of the afternoon passed in a blur as I tried to burn to my memory every precious moment so that it would stick with me on my new journey.

Families joined us at the end of the session, and we shared cake together. The kids ignored me for the most part, but I knew it was their way of dealing with their own own flood of emotions. And the upcoming change of therapist.

Beverly walked to me with her mother, and she offered me one of her paintings. The side profile of a child sniffing a daisy, done in orange and red paints only. It was beautiful.

"Thank you so much, Gavin," her mother said. "For everything. The gallery called earlier. They asked for two more of her paintings. She doesn't show it, but I know she'll miss you. We'll miss you too. I hope you'll come back to us one day. But what you're doing is priceless. As a mother, this is the most selfless thing someone could do for my daughter." She squeezed my forearm. "You're an angel."

They left, and a piece of my heart followed them.

———

Alone in my apartment, a beer bottle in hand, I stared at the city skyline in the far distance. Earlier, I went with a few of my colleagues to a bar downtown to celebrate the new chapter of my life—and my career. And my last day of work.

Now in the comfort of my home, in the dark, I felt more lonely than I had in a long time.

Every time I was left to my own thoughts, they traveled back to Playa De La Isla Azul. And Aisha Jones. The woman I missed every second of every day. The woman I would probably never be able to forget... Or get over.

The woman who had carved her name deep into my soul. Forever.

My breath hitched whenever images of us flickered in my mind.

Then a smile peeked out at the memory of my afternoon with the kids and all the progress they'd made since I started working with them.

Tonight, my feelings were a melting pot of hope, sadness, and gratitude. And love.

I dragged a hand over my face, unable to decide if I should cry or be happy as all my emotions stirred inside me.

Like I did almost every night, I looked at a picture of Aisha on New Year's Eve on my phone, wearing that red dress. Before everything went to shit. When her smile, pure and unfiltered, still brightened her face and everything around her. When we still had a chance to be something more than a vacation fling.

When I would have given my life to have one of her smiles aimed at me...or one last kiss. The one we never shared the way we should have. The one that should've been filled with wild passion and whispered promises.

The happiness I'd felt earlier dampened and only bitterness remained.

A few days ago, I heard one of her songs on the radio and was transported back to that first night we spent on the beach after I took her shopping. The night when we shared a part of our souls. I'd switched the station, not ready to hear her voice again—even if I craved it every night in my dreams.

With a shake of my head, I brought the bottle to my lips, chugging half of it.

I tipped my head back, staring at the ceiling. My last conversation with Gaston replayed in my head. Something that had been happening regularly since New Year's morning, when I woke up with a hangover on the beach.

Figure out what you want. Far from here. When you're back in your everyday life. And if Aisha is still the one, then fight for her. With everything you have.

It had been over three weeks now, and a lot had changed in my life since that day, but one thing remained constant. I missed Aisha. All of her. Her smile. Her affection. Her laughter. And her soft skin, her whimpers, and the way she made me feel. Whole. At peace. Handsome. And loved.

I missed looking at the starry sky like I did in Playa De La Isla Azul. Due to the city lights, I couldn't spot any from my living room window. But even if none were visible to the eyes, they were still there, watching over me. Watching over her. Every single one of them reminded me of the woman I lost.

"One day, soon, I'll come to get you, beautiful star. I need your light. And your love. One day, you'll stop fighting us. You'll let me in so I can show you just how amazing we are together."

The thought took roots in my heart and was enough to revive its dying parts.

I had no idea how I would get to her, but I was done giving her time to miss me. If I could change my career path in a matter of weeks, I could go after the woman I loved and show her that even after all this time, she was still the one every piece of me belonged to. The one it desired.

I had two weeks left before the beginning of my new adventure, and I had a flight to Michigan scheduled early the next morning. To spend a few days with Camilla and the boys. Make up for the missed holidays.

I watched the luggage piled by the door.

Maybe I could make a detour to Nashville on my way to Portland, and look up Aisha.

It would give me at least a week to find a way to sweep her off her feet. And to help her confront her fears, and make her trust me with the care of her heart.

My whole being sparked to life at the thought, as though I was breathing again for the first time.

I was about to embark on a new chapter in my life, and deep down, I hoped Aisha would be a part of it. That we could keep writing our story together, chapter after chapter, until we'd written the whole book.

I blew out a long breath. I could do this. I had to try one more time—to make her see that our time together wasn't over. That we could make it work. Yeah, I owed it to myself... to us. Because Aisha Jones was the only woman I fancied. And I wasn't known to be a quitter.

I inhaled. If I could drop everything for those kids, I should be able to do the same for my own happiness. Time to fight for what was mine—or should be mine—and get the girl back.

Now I just needed a plan… Oh yes, and a way to track her down.

Let's just hope she missed me as much as I'd missed her since we parted ways.

There was only one way to find out.

"I'll come find you, beautiful star. Wait for me."

Chapter 17

Aisha

I rang the doorbell, freezing on the front porch, rubbing my hands together. Why didn't I bring a warmer jacket? What was I thinking? I lived in Nashville—definitely not a winter wonderland—so the idea of that much cold and snow always caught me off guard.

Footsteps resonated on the other side of the door.

Angst filled me, and my insides seemed to swell and shrink just as fast.

My breath came out in billows of mist, thanks to the arctic temperatures.

Doubts crippled me. Was coming here a mistake? Maybe I should've thought the plan through a little longer before acting on it.

If I hurried, maybe I could leave before someone answered the door.

What was I thinking? I should have called first...or abandoned this ridiculous plan altogether. What was I thinking when I booked that flight? I must have been out of my mind. That was the only way to explain why I was standing here right now.

Think fast, Aisha.

I turned around, ready to leave, but the door swung open before I could make a run for it.

I'd been caught. A sigh escaped me as I readied myself for the inevitable.

A silhouette filled the doorway, and I blinked, certain I was dreaming. My lungs refused to draw air. I became dizzy.

"Aish…huh, Maggie? Wh-what are you doing here?" Gavin's deep voice jolted me out of my stunned silence.

I wrinkled my face, breathing through my nose, trying to calm the tsunami tearing through me. The storm that threatened to shatter me to pieces. His ocean and manly scent hit my nostrils, and I committed it all to memory.

My chest flipped with excitement. Gosh, I'd missed him so much.

"Hey, Gavin," I said with a small wave, probably looking ridiculous. "Sorry for coming by unannounced. I… When… It's just… I-I didn't… This was a bad idea. You'll think I'm being stupid. I, huh, should just leave."

I threw myself down the stairs, but Gavin grabbed my elbow from behind, halting my escape. Heat shot through me, and I thought I'd melt on the spot.

I willed my lungs to resume their function, pulling in a shaky breath.

Knots coiled around my stomach, and my body throbbed like a living drum.

"Mags, wait. Talk to me. Why are you here? Are you okay?"

The sound of his voice alone was enough to disrupt the flimsy balance I had created inside me in the last few weeks. A surge of warmth traveled from the crown of my head to the tips of my toes, and I relished the feeling.

"It's okay. Really. Don't worry. I'll go. I shouldn't have come. I didn't think this through."

Gavin pulled me to him, tipping my chin up with a finger, forcing me to meet his sky-blue eyes. The ones I'd dreamed about every night we'd been apart.

His lips were close. Too close. I tried to look away, but I had a hard time, the memories of all the kisses we'd shared pulling me in.

His gaze flickered between my eyes and my mouth, intensifying the ache I felt for him deep in my belly.

The longer he stared, the darker his irises grew. I blinked as I watched him. Smelled him. Felt him everywhere.

"Maggie, don't bullshit me. You're here. Tell me why you're here."

I sealed my lids, fighting my tears to stay at bay. "It's… it's complicated."

"It's me. Don't bullshit me. Not this time. You owe me an explanation. The last memory I have of you is on New Year's Eve, and it's a sour one."

I scratched the side of my head, gathering all my courage.

When did I become such a chickenshit? Oh yeah, since it involved my heart—amongst other things.

Gavin let go of me and crossed his arms over his broad chest. "Talk."

I took a deep, shaky breath, missing the feel of his touch.

"Remember the day you took me shopping because I only had snowflake and reindeer clothes to wear?" He nodded. "Well, I-I promised I'd invite you to dinner. I'm here…I'm here to follow up on my words. I'm sorry it took me so long."

Gavin gave me a sharp look, scratching his scruffy jaw.

Dark shadows lined his eyes. His hair was longer and messier than I recalled. It was still a good look on him, though. It suited him. He watched me with a frown. His skin, golden from the sun, looked paler surrounded by that white scenery. His blue eyes twinkled for a few short seconds, bringing me back to Playa De La Isla Azul—and to everything we once were.

Soon, sadness swirled in them, chasing the memories away.

Guilt stabbed me like a sudden, sharp pain. It hurt more than anything else I'd ever felt. Looking at him, I missed his easy smile and contagious happiness. Did I do that to him? Steal his light?

Did I hurt him so bad we would never be able to go back to what we once were?

Gavin studied me. I had no idea how I imagined our reunion to be, but in my head, I'd wished he would sweep me off my feet and kiss me senseless. Who was I kidding? He probably hated me for what I did and how I drove him away.

Thanks for the reality check, life. Fairytales don't exist. No need to rub it in my face.

"You came all the way to Michigan because you owed me dinner?" His clipped words crushed my wishful heart, sinking it to my toes. Heat vanished from my body, turning me into an icicle. Who knew Michigan winters were this brutal? "Not interested."

My shoulders sagged forward, and my insides turned to mush.

All the hope I wore as a shield, whispering that I could fix the relationship I'd screwed up like a boss, died.

Hugging myself with my arms, I stood there, frozen, unable to speak.

Gavin's shoulders dropped, mirroring mine.

We held each other's gaze, neither of us brave enough to break the awkward silence filling the crispy air between us.

Trying hard not to break into tears, I pinched my lips into a thin line and blinked the moisture away. "Okay, then," I finally said. "I hope you have a great life… I-I'm sorry for bothering you. Goodbye, Gavin." I whirled around, but he clutched my upper arm before I could reach the steps. "What? What do you want from me?"

His face inched toward mine, emotions flickering in his eyes. I felt myself dissolve under the heat of his smoldering gaze. How could he still have that much effect on me?

"You came all this way for me?"

I nodded. Or shrugged. Maybe both. Everything felt kind of surreal right now. My words caught in my throat, and I felt as if I would drown in my own feelings if I spoke.

"You came all this way only to see me?"

I glanced down at my shoes, not warm enough for the cold weather. Then raised my eyes to meet his.

Why was I having such a hard time dealing with my feelings? Why couldn't I just tell Gavin everything I'd rehearsed for hours since I woke up this morning? Why was it so hard to be honest with him…and with myself?

Gavin spoke first, and I swallowed the anxiety ball bouncing up and down my throat. "Mags, I don't want you to repay your debt because I'm not that guy. No dinner, okay? Forget it…" He drew in a sharp breath. "Unless you're here to give me a chance. To give *us* a chance."

The silence lasted half a second but felt like an eternity.

"I've been thinking about you nonstop since you left

Las Palmeras. I've replayed what we shared in my head more times than I can count. There's only one verdict: I'm obsessed with you, Aisha Jones. I'm in love with you. If you're here, I'm pretty sure it's because you've missed me too. What we had transformed me. I did not find my Christmas spirit back because my sister sent me on that vacation. I found it because I met you. And you showed me miracles exist, and good things could happen during the holidays."

I blinked fast.

"I wanna be with you, Mags."

I stilled, everything inside me coming to a halt.

"And brace yourself, I have news. I somehow quit my job two days ago."

His words woke me up from my stupor. I jerked back, not sure if I heard him right. "You did what? Why?" The lining of my throat itched. I couldn't breathe or swallow anymore. Nothing made sense.

Was I still on the plane and dreaming?

Gavin's voice pulled me from the haze into the present, steadying my racing thoughts.

"Well, not a full-on quit… More like a sabbatical… A friend of mine is organizing conferences all over the country, and I've decided to join him on a two-month tour."

"A tour?"

"Yeah. Like you, but different… To raise awareness for kids on the autism spectrum. And get funding, so they can access the treatments and care they need. Those families already endure so much… The last thing they need is the added burden of financial stress."

"Gavin… Wow. I-I'm speechless. That's amazing. I already knew you were someone exceptional, but this really seals the deal. You'll be great at it. I just…I just know it."

"Thanks. It's all new territory, but I believe it's worth it. Those kids are worth it."

"What about leaving them behind? Aren't you sad? Deep down, I'm sure it must have been a tough decision to make."

"Dr. Kauffman will take good care of them. We've been working together for a long time. They are used to him. They'll be okay. I'll come see them every chance I get." He swallowed and continued. "Wait, there's more. I have something to tell you… When I returned to Boston, after you know… Nothing felt right in my life anymore, no matter how much I tried to get over you. Everything had lost all its magic. Sherry, my sister's wife, has friends in the music industry in Nashville. I was about to use her connections to track you down."

"You were? Why?"

"Because I love you, Aisha Jones. And I've missed you like crazy. I wanna be with you. Not just for a two-week vacation, but every day of my life, if we can make it work. My soul is sad when you're not around. As if it's missing its other half. Our attraction…our chemistry…our bond… they're stronger than us. In a way I can't explain, I feel I've known you all my life and we were destined to meet in Playa De La Isla Azul. I haven't changed my mind since New Year's Eve. In my heart, I'm still certain we belong together."

The river flowing down my face turned to icicles in the frigid winter air. I sobbed in silence, my shoulders heaving.

"Fuck, you're gonna freeze to death," Gavin said, pulling me into his arms and leading me inside. His warmth poured into me, thawing the frost that had settled in my heart and giving me the comfort I'd been trying so hard to deny myself. "Mags, say something."

I smiled through my tears as Gavin watched me, waiting for me to speak.

"Gavin, I…huh, I messed up. Big time. I'm here, freezing my ass off, hoping I'm not too late and hoping you'll give me a second chance. Hoping you still want me." My tears burned the back of my eyes. "I'm sorry… I really am. For-for everything. I was wrong. The truth is… What I'm really trying to say is... I love you. I knew I did back then, but I was too afraid to admit it, even to myself. To be honest, this scares the shit out of me. You came into my life and rocked my world, and I wasn't ready to admit my feelings for you that night. But I'm a mess since I left you on that beach and broke your heart. Now I can't sleep because I think about you all the time." I paused, trying to sort through my thoughts. "Gavin, I-I lied to you."

He didn't move as I stepped closer, leaving only a hair's breadth between our bodies. Could he hear the rapid pounding in my veins and read my deepest thoughts? Would he still want me after all the hurtful things I said? Even though none of them were true, and I'd just opened my heart to him?

I stared into his eyes, letting him see it was my heart doing all the talking. "I'm not just here to treat you to dinner. I-I'm here to tell you I want this with you… Love. A relationship. The whole nine yards. I'm ready for you… for *us*. I need you in my life, Gavin. Because everything is shinier and better when you're by my side. We'll find a way, okay? To make it work. If I must travel back and forth between Boston—or wherever you are—and Nashville daily, I will. Nothing will keep me away from you ever again."

Gavin framed my face with his strong hands. "Mags, do you know how many times I've wished to hear you say those words? So many times, that I lost count."

The tangled knot of emotions in my chest bounced around, getting bigger every time Gavin spoke.

"Is leaving your job what you really want? Don't you need to think it through some more? You don't need to rush into anything because you need a change. I'm not going anywhere this time. That is, if you'll have me."

"Mags, I love working with those kids, but I think I can help them even more by fighting for them. At least, for now. They need me. They need someone to show the world how special they are. I think I'm the man for the job." He paused. "But there's more. I crave you. Every minute of every day. Every minute of the night. I want an *us*. You live under my skin, and I don't want you to ever go away. You've already stolen my heart, and I never want you to give it back."

"You sure?"

"Positive. I'm done waiting for you to change your mind. I'm all about showing you what you've been missing by being too stubborn. We owe it to ourselves to have a chance… A real one. I even had a plan."

"You did?"

"Yeah. To go to Nashville, find you, and seduce you. To sweep you off your feet, because you deserve nothing less. And then to make love to you and remind you of all the things we could be…or should be. Of all the things we are when we're together. And how perfect you are for me."

"You did? You wanted to pursue me?"

"If you still had no idea, I'll tell you this. I would do just about anything for you. That's how much I'm sure you're the one for me."

I wiped my tears with the tips of my fingers. My voice quivered as I spoke. "I feared you would push me away. That…that you would have moved on…or changed your mind."

"Mags, why do you keep listening to your fears? They've been nothing but wrong since day one. They prevent you from living life fully. There's so much I want to tell you…so much I wanna share with you. So much has happened in the last few days. Let's get dinner before my sister and her children come back. Once they meet you, they'll fall in love with you too, and you'll be stuck with us forever. In the Moore family, when we love, it's pretty deep. There is no escape."

I let out a heartfelt laugh. Gavin laced our fingers together.

"Wait? How did you find me? How did you know I'd be here today?"

"Your sister."

He pointed to his chest. "*My* sister?"

"She sent an email to Riley, my manager, just when I realized how big of a fool I'd been and wanted to look for you myself…because I did. I had a plan of my own to track you down. Anyway, your sister said she had no idea how I did it, but that the time we spent together had changed you. For the better. And she wanted to thank me."

"She did?"

I nodded. "Guess her wife's connections are good after all."

Gavin rubbed the skin of his nape. "Impressive. I had no clue she did that. Wow… I'm speechless."

I moved closer. "She loves you. A lot. We chatted back and forth a few times. I confided in her that I missed you and wanted to make it up to you. She told me you would be here this afternoon, alone, so I seized the chance."

"Okay. So, she lied about having an appointment with the kids."

I nodded.

"She tricked me."

I nodded again.

"If I agree to have dinner with you, will you run away when things get serious?"

I shook my head.

"What made you change your mind?"

"Many things. One day, I was in the studio, recording a new song, and the lyrics… I don't know, they woke up something inside me. They spoke of you. Of us. And what I had lost. Something I was trying hard to ignore. The way Carter sang that chorus, his voice, I don't know. The pain… It-it sounded as if he had lost the love of his life. It reminded me of everything we were during the holidays… and everything I've lost. It reminded me of what you said that night…" I coughed to clear my throat. "After…after I told you those awful things. The memories of every second we spent together strangled my chest until I couldn't breathe. I broke down that day, knowing how much of a fool I'd been. Later that night, I joined my friends for dinner, trying to distract myself from everything that had happened. They were all so blissfully happy. It-it hit me. I wanted what they had. Love. Someone to share my life with. *You.* I had you, but I walked away. I regret every hurtful thing I said to you back on that beach, Gavin. I'm so *so* sorry. If you let me, I'll spend the rest of my life showing you I'm in this for good. You were right. I should have listened to my heart that night… It told me many times to shut the fuck up and stop fighting you, but I didn't listen—" My voice cracked on the last word.

"Are you really sure it's what you want? That I'm what you want? Because you're here, and I'm not ready to let you go again. We have weeks to make up for."

I gazed at our joined hands. "This time, I'm not going away. I'm ready to fight for you. And for what we could be."

"Good, because there are things I wanna do to you—with you—before we go out. These weeks without you have been hard." My lips stretched into a sad smile, and I bowed my head. He planted a kiss on my forehead, and I melted a little inside. "Remember that first night we spent together?" His eyes shimmered with unconcealed desire, washing away my uneasiness.

I nodded, every nerve inside me coming alive, a deep ache building in my lower belly. "What do you have in mind?"

"I'm sure we can find a Santa hat in the basement… and maybe ice cubes. Let's re-enact that night because the memory of it has been spicing up my dreams for weeks now. For the longest time, I thought I would never get a do-over. Please, Mags, show me how wrong I've been." Gavin's voice, dripping with love—and lust—heated up my entire body. All my cells tingled with anticipation.

"You sure? We could wait for the Easter bunny to make an appearance instead. I'm sure I'd look cute with ears and a tail."

"Nah. Right now, it's Mrs. Claus I want. Naked in my bed."

I quirked an eyebrow. "Is that so?"

He bobbed his head several times, that mischievous smirk of him tugging at his lips.

"In this case, show me the way, Santa."

"Fuck, I love it when you talk dirty." We both burst out laughing.

Gavin grew serious after a moment. My pulse sped up. Why was he staring at me this way? A wild flutter raced through me. Without another word, Gavin pressed me against the hallway wall and crashed his lips on mine. The same addictive taste of him that I missed heightened all my senses. The scent of him filled my nose. And every corner of my heart.

Our tongues met and danced that tango we'd rehearsed many times together before.

His mouth made love to mine, promising me we'd be okay. That we'd work it out. He pressed his forehead against mine and stared right into my soul, his chest rising and falling in quick pants.

"I love you, Mags. Don't leave the next time you're having doubts. Just talk to me. We're a team. We'll figure it out. Together."

I bobbed my head. "I love you."

My mouth searched his, and I dissolved against his warm embrace.

This. This moment. This moment right here.

How could I have lived weeks without Gavin in my life?

He was right when he said we knew each other from beyond this life. I felt it in my bones as he lifted me in his arms, his mouth still fused to mine, our heartbeats syncing and every worry melting away.

I was where I belonged. My heart was where it belonged too.

Epilogue
Aisha

Eleven months later

"You sure you're ready for this?" Gavin asked between searing kisses. The ones I'd become addicted to and now couldn't even imagine living without.

I nodded. "Yeah. As long as we're together, I can face my fears."

"Okay, then let's do this."

We exited the golf-cart shuttle fifteen minutes later, and they all waited for us in the lobby, welcoming us with champagne flutes and contagious grins.

"You came. I knew you would," Ruth exclaimed, dressed in a red dress with golden trims. "Come here, dear." She tugged at my hand. "We need to talk business. And by the way, that smile you put on Mr. Gavin's face, it suits him well."

I let out a loud laugh. "Show me the way, Ruth. But can I have one of those first?" I asked, gesturing to her glass.

"Sure. Gaston will fetch you some."

Gavin kissed my cheek before letting go of my other hand.

Love you, he mouthed.

Warmth surged through me, and I had no idea how I ever turned my back on him a year ago.

"What's the plan?" I asked Ruth.

Her eyes shone brighter. "Christmas tree and sand snowmen contests. Wreath creation workshop. And eggnog tasting. Is that too much? When Mr. Gavin wrote to me a few weeks ago, he told me you were ready to get your holiday groove back. Since you're here only for a few days, we better make the most of it."

I nodded while squeezing her hand. "It's more than fine. Thank you." I lowered my voice. "Don't tell Gavin, but I even got us matching Christmas sweaters. My aunt makes those. I'd like to surprise him on Christmas morning."

Ruth winked at me. "Your secret is safe with me"—she winked again—"*Maggie.*"

I snickered. "Thanks." My eyes drifted to the man I couldn't wait to have a taste of—the plane ride had been way too long for our liking—and my fingers ached to touch every inch of him. I brought my attention back to the old lady by my side. "If you could excuse us, we're going to settle in. We'll meet you later for dinner."

Gavin and I reached our room, barely able to keep our hands off each other.

"God, Mags. I love you. I can't believe we're here again. It's like a déjà-vu but with a happy ending this time."

He always called me *Mags* in private or when we were out. Even though I knew people often recognized me, it felt like we lived in a world of our own, a secret just between us.

I wrapped my arms around his neck and tugged him down for a kiss. "It's our own little tradition. I'm glad we're back. It may take me some time to adjust to all this Christmassy, but I'm not hiding this year. Truth? I'm actually looking forward to our first official Christmas morning together."

"You are?" I nodded. "What about our first Christmas vacation lovemaking? I don't think you need time to adjust to that. I even packed the Santa hat for the occasion."

My body vibrated at Gavin's words. As if on cue, his hands reached for my sweater, and he peeled it over my head. His eyes drew me in, and I liquified, right in front of him.

"Love me," I begged. "Because we're not exiting this room all day."

———

Ten days later

The crowd cheered and applauded. My entire body lit up, relishing the addictive energy surrounding me. I breathed out. For years, I'd turned down this opportunity. And now I was here, about to do something I never thought I would ever do again.

First, a vacation at Las Palmeras, and now this.

Carter Hills, Nashville's most beloved country music star, neared me. We hadn't sung together onstage in years.

"Ready for this craziness?" he asked, kissing my cheek.

"I think so."

"Aisha, I'm glad that man of yours drilled some sense into your head, and you accepted to join me. I don't do many big concerts anymore, so this means a lot to me."

I squeezed my friend's forearm. "I'm happy we're doing it together. I'm not sure I would have been ready to do this on my own just yet. It may take me some time to get the whole Christmas-is-magical thing going strong."

Carter gripped my hand. "We're in this together, and we've rehearsed that song of yours many times. We'll be just fine."

I bowed my hand. I knew he was right. He was Carter Hills, for God's sake.

"Let's do this."

"New York's end-of-the-year ball drop celebration is underway. Get ready to rock this stage," Riley said, nearing us. "You guys are the best." He turned to face me. "Everything will be all right, kiddo."

I nodded and breathed in—and out. Yeah, I could do this. Carter and I walked onstage, and a surge of emotion filled me to the brim.

"How is it going, New York?" I hollered at the crowd, unable to wipe the grin off my face. "It's my first time being part of the Times Square New Year's Eve celebration. Please help me make this experience one to remember."

Carter winked as he started playing the first chord of "Lost and Found."

Gavin captured my attention when my attention drifted to the side of the stage.

We were lost. We were alone.
But life brought us
together.
We were lost. We were sad. But

it's over 'cause we belong together.

———

"I thought Sam was joining us? I thought he'd be here tonight." I asked Carter when we walked offstage a little after midnight, adrenaline coursing and buzzing in my veins.

Riley met us, handing us bottles of water we were more than grateful for. He shook his head, and his smile dropped a little. "I tried to bring him onboard. I really did. He's not returning my calls. He doesn't have a managing team anymore, so I have to deal with him directly. Even though he's one of my best friends, he still doesn't confide in me about everything. His wife abandoning him and his daughters has shattered all his dreams. I saw them the other day… The girls are doing okay, but Sam is a mess. I'm worried about him. He's not the man we used to know."

"Yeah, I saw him too and barely recognized him," Carter chimed in. "He has lost the spark in his eyes. It's fucking sad, if you ask me. Sam's a good man….and a true legend. He didn't deserve any of this."

Riley clapped both our shoulders. "Let's give him more time, okay? And then I'll bring him back. I have no idea how or when, but I will. We'll get him to join our team, and I hope he'll stop resisting the idea of working with me and trust that I'll have his back. Anyway, I have a plan. You'll see, kids."

"You always do," I said.

"Yes, and that's why I'm the best." He hugged us both. "I'm proud of you, guys. And I'm happy you're finally doing this with us, Aisha. It was about damn time."

Backstage, Gavin strode in my direction, lifted me in

his arms, and twirled me around. "Happy New Year, my love. So proud of you, Mags. You're my star. Now and forever. Let's go home."

The End

————

Thank you for reading Aisha and Gavin's emotional and beautiful love story.

Curious about Sam Stevens?
Pick up your copy of Fallen Legend

emmanuellesnow.com/products/fallen-legend

————

FREE bonus chapter
Want even more? Your bonus chapter awaits here
emmanuellesnow.com

————

Carter and April's story: read False Promises
Riley and Devon's story: read Last Hope
Dahlia and Nick's story: read Cruel Destiny
Sam and Maddie's story: read Fallen Legend

ACKNOWLEDGMENTS

The Holidays are all about being grateful, and this year I have so much to be thankful for.

The year has been a wonderful ride that I'd only pictured in my wildest dreams but had no idea how to make it happen. One day, I woke up and decided go for it. And it happened. In more ways than I could have ever imagined. A milestone in my life was this year, where people came and went, but every one of them taught me some valuable lesson in their own way.

To all of you, I want to say thank you. For helping to make my dream happen. For being there with me all through.

Firstly, thank you, my awesome readers, for your love and trust; this is an incredible feeling no word can truly express. Because of you, I do what I love, and my heart vibrates every time you laugh, smile, and cry while you immerse yourself in one of my stories.

Thank you to my own squad, my little team, who believes in me and enjoys every step of my author journey with enthusiasm, showing so much confidence in me. My four babies, I'm the luckiest mama in the world to have you in my corner. Thank you to Mr. Snow, who has always believed in me and given me the chance to do what I was born to do, standing tall by my side since day one. You said I could do it, and you were right. I'll forever be grateful.

Thanks to my ARC team who falls in love with my stories, but mostly with my characters. I lay my heart down in every line, every plot twist, every emotion. I shed tears along the way, crying for their losses and also their victories, big or small. I laugh and smile, cheer on them and push them to be bigger and better people. Live through their flaws and follow their hearts. I'm grateful that you guys love my characters as if they were your friends and families too. This means a lot to me.

Thank you to the bloggers and bookstagrammers who share my books. It brings a smile to my face and warmth in my heart every time I see those posts. It's a wonderful feeling.

A special and huge thank you to Shalini. There's so much I could tell you today. I set myself up for two Christmas stories this Holiday season, but ended up unable to tame my creativity (and my word count) and delivered more than I thought I could. You were there in every step of the way, cheering on me and pushing me to pour my heart in my words. And the final result is what love stories are all about.

I couldn't have done it without you. And I'm grateful life put you on my journey. You're the best! And you know what, we did it! Even when I gave you short deadlines, and my document kept adding words at night.

This is a story of a second chance unconditional love and hope for forever.

And I wish it warms your heart and makes you believe in soulmates too.

Emmanuelle

ABOUT THE AUTHOR

Soulfully Beautiful Love Stories

USA Today Bestselling author Emmanuelle Snow is a contemporary author of mature YA and New Adult love stories, who gives life to strong characters who'll fight with all they have to reach their life goals and find their own happiness.

Emmanuelle is in love with love. Especially complicated, deep, and passionate feelings that make a relationship extraordinary and complex all at the same time.

In her spare time, when she's not writing or reading, she likes to go on road trips—with her four kids and her own soulmate—watch movies, paint, or do some DIY, always with a cup of green tea in her hand and listening to country music.

She splits her time between beautiful Canada and the small US towns she adores.

Find all of Emmanuelle's books here:
emmanuellesnow.com

———

Want to connect with Emmanuelle online?

ALSO BY THE AUTHOR

CARTER HILLS BAND UNIVERSE

(suggested reading order)

Carter Hills Band series

False Promises

Heart Song Duet

Blindsided

Forevermore

Whiskey Melody series

Sweet Agony

Second Tear Duet

Cruel Destiny

Beautiful Salvation

Breathless Duet

Wild Encounter

Brittle Scars

Upon A Star Series

Last Hope

Midnight Sparks

Love Song For Two Series

Read them all

emmanuellesnow.com

All available on author's bookshop

EMMANUELLE

USA TODAY BESTSELLING AUTHOR

SNOW

FALLEN LEGEND

a love story

Love Song for Two series - book one

FALLEN LEGEND

SAM

Fisting my hands at my sides, I paced the room, a ball of lightning bouncing around my chest. This was a nightmare. A disaster about to happen. How had I not seen this one coming? How could I have been so blind?

My nails dug trenches in my palms, drawing pinpricks of blood, but I would keep my composure. I had to.

The lump in my larynx rubbed against the chaffed walls of my throat.

I reeled in some of my wrath and tried another approach. My voice came out a ragged whisper, but calmer this time, putting my pride to rest. And urging my sanity to stay in the game. "Lisa, you can't be serious. Listen, there must be something *I* can do. Can we talk about it first? And what about the kids? How am I going to explain any of this to them? We'll get help... You can't just leave like this."

No emotions—rather not the ones I wished to see—crossed her hardened features. No *I'm having second thoughts.* Or *you might be right, we'll get help.*

My wife had turned to stone, unmoving and unreadable.

Hoping the pain would numb the one ripping my chest in two, I tugged at the roots of my hair. How could I have been so clueless about the woman I'd been married to for the last four years?

She pushed another shirt into her bag, ignoring my words.

Maybe I could reach out to the mother inside her. "Lisa, your leaving will fuck them up for the rest of their lives. Abandoning your own children, really? That's not what motherhood is all about." I halted and turned around to face the woman, who I thought I knew so well, zipping up her royal-blue suitcase. The one that had traveled around the world with us for years. Yeah, what a joke.

She finally raised her gaze, and I saw determination pass through her eyes this time. She wasn't doubting her decision to walk away from us, her family. I studied her for a long minute, wishing I could see tears glistening somewhere in them, or regret marring her features. But there were none.

She was done.

When did my wife harbor a rock in place of her heart?

"Is it about the miscarriages?" I asked, praying she'd say yes and that I could call her doctor and set up an appointment to discuss her psychological distress. "I know how difficult it's been on you, but it's been hard on me too. We can get through this. Together. We're a good team. We love each other."

She sighed and shook her head, her eyes still showing no sign of hurt or sadness. Or anything. "That's the thing, Sam. I don't love you. I did. Once. But both miscarriages were eye-opening. I need to find myself. I'm twenty-eight. For the last six years, I've followed you around the globe. I liked that. For the last four, I've played wife and mommy. And I enjoyed it…at some point. Being a parent is your thing. We had babies because you wanted to be a daddy… I never asked to be a mother. In all honesty, I thought it'd grow on me…" She shrugged. "But it didn't. I crave fresh air. To be free to do whatever I want. Whenever I want it. And being a parent isn't just what I hoped it'd be. I'm sorry, but I'm over it."

I blinked. What? Was she serious right now? *She's over it?*

I was having one of those crippling nightmares that felt too much like reality. This was it. No woman in her right mind would say such horrible things about her own children. About her family.

Her flesh.

Her blood.

My Adam's apple bobbed, and bile rose in my throat. Tinted with disgust and disdain.

My wife was delusional.

Who should I call to get her some help?

Could her state of mind be ruled a mental breakdown? Did she require psychiatric professionals? Or a vacation? No matter what, she looked sane.

Lisa smiled at me as if quitting on us was just a daily occurrence and not something about to wreck our entire world.

My shoulders fell, and so did my heart. I inched closer when she moved to her feet. "Can we talk about this? Please. You at least owe me that. We've been through so much together. Did you forget everything?" I asked, forcing my voice to sound even, trying my best to keep my anger under wraps.

She offered me another twist of her lips. This time, she

looked diabolical. Who was this woman? Where did my wife go?

"I owe you nothing, Sammy. The ride has been fun, but I'm not playing this family game anymore. I'm out. Oh, and I'll send you the divorce papers in a week or two."

My eyes sprang wider.

What the actual fuck?

"Divorce papers? Don't you think it's a little early to talk about divorce? We haven't even fought about anything serious in the past, and now you're talking about dissolving our marriage. Tell me you're kidding. Where are the cameras? The crew? Is it for a celebrity prank TV show?"

My wife—or soon-to-be ex-wife if she had her way—huffed, as if anything I said sounded childish. Asking her to stay seemed to scrape on her nerves.

"C'mon, Sammy. I'm moving to the other side of the world. I won't return. Ever. Come to terms with it. Nothing you do or say will change anything." She sighed again and shook her head, looking desperate. "I. Am. Not. Coming. Back. Ever. This"—she pointed around the room with her finger—"is over. You and I, we're done." A car honked outside. "Now move, my cab is waiting." She pushed past me, rolling her suitcase behind her.

I stood there, frozen. None of this made sense. The dream had lasted long enough. I could wake up now. *Please make this nightmare go away.*

Read Sam Steven's story,
Fallen Legend, now

emmanuellesnow.com/fallen-legend

Author's bookstore at emmanuellesnowshop.com

"Emmanuelle Snow doesn't just tell a story, she creates an entire world." (ReadaholicDeb)

"Emmanuelle Snow has done it again! This powerful, heartwarming, slow-burn love story will break your heart on page one and slowly piece it back together. (Goodreads)

Fallen Legend is book one in the
Lonesome Heart duet.

emmanuellesnow.com/fallen-legend